HOLY TREASURE

When he got near the bottom, the constable turned on his torch again and squatted beside what from above had looked like a bundle of clothes splayed over the lowest steps. Now the bundle was revealed as the inert body of a woman. She was lying face downwards, neck bent at an unnatural angle, the clothing around the neck saturated with blood.

Careful about what he touched, the constable was trying for a pulse at the woman's wrist.

'Ambulance, Charlie,' he called up to his partner, 'but I think she's a goner.' His light caught the glint of something in the woman's right hand. The right arm was half extended. The object in the hand was an open clasp knife...

HOLY TREASURE

David Williams

ARROW BOOKS

Arrow Books Limited
20 Vauxhall Bridge Road, London SW1V 2SA

An imprint of Random Century Group

London Melbourne Sydney Auckland Johannesburg
and agencies throughout the world

First published in Great Britain 1989
by Macmillan London Ltd
Arrow edition 1991

Printed and bound in Great Britain by
Cox & Wyman Ltd, Reading

ISBN 0 09 971630 5

This one for
Barry Pike

Chapter One

'There were no baptisms or confirmations at Saint Martin's for the whole of last year? None at all? Nor for the year before?' the Area Bishop for West London demanded incredulously from his seat at the head of the table. He looked at the other three present as though seriously seeking a denial, except at this stage he could scarcely have been expecting one.

'Saint Martin's has become somewhat isolated,' said the Archdeacon, then loudly hissed in breath through stretched, open lips. This wasn't intended further to mark the unpalatable facts – only to ease the speaker's new dentures now brought into prominent display.

'A rural paradise, is it? In the heart of London?'

'I was speaking figuratively, Bishop.'

'So you don't mean there's no one living in Kengrave Square any more?' the Bishop enquired further with a sardonic glance at Miss Chorlton on his right. She responded with a twitchy half-smile.

'Hardly that, Bishop,' said Lancelot Tinder on the Bishop's left, and who happened to live in Kengrave Square himself.

'No weddings either, I see,' the Bishop commented with a frown that could have been accusing. 'Let's hope that accounts for the absence of baptisms too.'

Miss Chorlton, the Bishop's middle-aged secretary, delicately fastened the top button of her cardigan, an action that was hardly prompted by the dictates of decorum. The garment was being worn over a high-necked jumper which she had also knitted herself. Simply, Miss Chorlton – a spare body in several senses – was again noticing the draught in the Bishop's study.

'And are there really only nineteen people on the electoral roll?' The Bishop pulled his nose, which was long, like his chin. He had returned to studying the Pastoral Committee Report on the table in front of him.

'Eighteen people to be exact. One died recently. Most of the others live outside the parish,' said the Archdeacon earnestly, as though the last fact might well have accounted for their survival. He was plump and elderly, with an attitude that usually struck others as more definably philosophical than overtly religious. Certainly a long period in the job had inured him to alleged evidences of pastoral failure. 'You'll see the average Sunday attendance is twenty-four,' he went on, with a hint of pride that hardly seemed justified: there were three thousand people living in the parish of St Martin's of whom more than half had probably been formally received into the Church of England at some time or other. 'That's the total for all services, of course,' the speaker added from his seat on the other side of Miss Chorlton. 'It's not a good situation, but one we'd hoped was not entirely beyond redeeming.'

'Why? Seems to have been getting worse for years,' said the Bishop promptly. A slim ascetic, much younger than the Archdeacon, he was sharp in speech as well as feature, and new to the area as well as to the 'purple'.

Both clerics were good men according to their lights, but their outlooks were markedly different.

The Bishop required the churches in his care to be profit centres, with the annual net surplus measured in souls reclaimed. In addition, he expected – almost demanded – that there should be no backsliding on financial obligations on the part of parochial church councils.

In contrast, the Archdeacon thought of churches as 'symbols of continuity in an ocean of change' – monuments to the Almighty whom he expected to be accounting to in person before very long. On Judgement Day, he would be prepared to admit failing to convert enough souls during his and their brief sojourn on earth. Owning up to the abandonment of large, enduring buildings dedicated to the glory of an examining Deity was an entirely different matter.

It was the likely ultimate abandonment of St Martin's Church in Kengrave Square that the Committee Report was all about – the Report which was now being presented to the Bishop by two representative members of that Committee.

'The church has always met its financial obligations. To the parish and the diocese,' said the Archdeacon, aware of the new Bishop's strictures.

'That's largely due to the generosity of one person,' supplied Tinder, sitting up even straighter in his chair. He brushed both sides of his slim moustache with a straight forefinger – a persistent habit that disturbed Miss Chorlton sitting immediately opposite. Many assumed that Tinder's dapper appearance and clipped way of speaking were residues of a military background. He encouraged the impression, though he had never been in the army.

'You mean the generosity of this Mrs Lodey?' the Bishop questioned.

'Correct, Bishop. The Honourable Mrs Lodey. She was the daughter of a viscount. The First Lord Grenwood.' As a solicitor, Tinder was a stickler for exactness: as a social climber, he was also good on titles, and coveted one for himself.

Lancelot Tinder was the owner of a small legal practice in the area. He had inherited the firm from his father. He preferred to style himself as the senior partner, although the only other one was an ageing specialist in conveyancing, employed at a very low salary. Since the profitable conveyancing of domestic property made up the bulk of the firm's business, Tinder was able to leave most of the work to the other man and to an even less costly articled clerk. In this way, he could concentrate on his investments, and on what others perceived as his good works. The last were mostly activities calculated to show him indirect monetary gain, or else to strengthen his expectation of a knighthood – or to do both. He was a borough councillor, and a member of the Church of England General Synod. A number of other offices stemmed from these two. He was also chairman of a clutch of local charities.

Today, Tinder was present as deputy chairman of the Diocesan Pastoral Committee. Every diocese, or area diocese, has such a committee. It is the body that recommends to a bishop whether or not a church should be made redundant.

'So, without Mrs Lodey, the church could have been up for the chop before this?'

'Very possibly, Bishop,' agreed the Archdeacon, while deploring the other's choice of phrase, as well as the implication that money was the prime criterion.

'And the Committee have consulted all the interested parties?'

The Bishop was here using 'interested parties' in a statutory sense. Under the Pastoral Measure Act, all 'interested parties' – which, paradoxically though legally, has to include a number of uninterested ones – have to be consulted before a Pastoral Committee can recommend a redundancy. Once it has done so, and if the Bishop approves, it then asks the Church Commissioners for England to arrange for the designated church to be declared as no longer required for worship.

'We've been through all the motions most meticulously I'm afraid,' offered the Archdeacon, who was chairman of the Committee. Tinder was its senior lay member.

'And you were unanimous, you say?'

'Reluctantly, yes, Bishop,' offered the Archdeacon who had been the only waverer out of the Committee's seven members. 'There are some dissenting voices amongst the interested parties.'

'But none that will have any standing later? At Church Commissioners stage?' The Bishop paused: it was usual to get some opposition. 'The churchwardens aren't putting up a fight then?'

The Archdeacon eyed Lancelot Tinder expectantly across the table, but without saying anything himself.

Tinder cleared his throat. 'My wife is the churchwarden. The only one at the moment. I thought you knew that, Bishop.'

'Sorry, Lancelot. You had told me. And your wife isn't putting up a . . . I mean opposing the recommendation?' The Bishop gave a brief embarrassed smile.

Miss Chorlton's flagging interest was rekindled. She had been staring through the window at the leafless trees outside the Bishop's house on Camden Hill. She turned her gaze inward, unfortunately just in time to catch Tinder smooth his moustache again. Many years before, her late mother had counselled Miss Chorlton not to trust men with narrow moustaches. Also men who wore brown suits. Tinder was presently offending on both counts. Involuntarily, Miss Chorlton's legs meshed together under the table even more tightly than before.

'Enid, my wife, has been in two minds,' Tinder was responding, oblivious to the disquiet he was causing opposite. 'But I think we can safely assume she's now come round to the sensible view.'

Miss Chorlton's thin, unpainted lips firmed in a sign of suppressed contempt.

'Enid's fond of the place. Naturally, we both are,' Tinder continued with increasing volume and as though he were addressing a public meeting. He tended to do this when he was less than sure of his ground. Miss Chorlton had noticed as much at other meetings. 'Enid's been very good about regular attendance. Sense of obligation, of course. Case of divided loyalty though. In recent months our family allegiance has transferred to Saint Winifred's, Nelson Gardens. They've invited me to become a sidesman there.'

Miss Chorlton's eyebrows lifted a fraction. Family allegiance might be expected to be somewhat greater at the church where one member of the family was churchwarden than at one where another member was a mere sidesman – unless the lesser office happened to be held by Lancelot Tinder, and unless Lancelot Tinder had plans for promotion.

'And there really is no argument for keeping Saint Martin's going,' Tinder continued. 'The parish is quite the smallest in the area. That's in geographical size as well as population. It was small, even in Victorian times. Should never have been instituted as a parish in the first place.'

'When was it instituted?' enquired the Bishop.

'In 1874,' Tinder supplied. 'Carved out of the corners of three adjacent parishes. There was a good deal of protest at the time. To the Bishop of London. He let it go through though. Great mistake,' he ended pointedly, as though to warn this bishop not to persist in the episcopal errors of the previous century.

'The protest would have been from the clergy in the other parishes. Not wanting to lose fat fees and fatter congregations,' the Bishop observed ruefully: those were the days. 'Private church was it?'

'Yes, and High.' This was the Archdeacon. 'So there was liturgical objection as well. Saint Martin's was meant to counteract the proliferation of estate churches at the time. It was very High.' He wasn't referring to the physical height of the church building, but to the forms of worship used at St Martin's. These had been in the High Church or Anglo-Catholic tradition, though they were not so much today. The Archdeacon was himself a High Churchman, while the Bishop was the opposite – an Evangelical.

'All those estate churches were Evangelical, of course,' said the Bishop. 'Had to be.'

The estates referred to had been builders' estates. From

early Victorian times, the railways had induced a massive westward shift of better-off Londoners. The rash of builders' estates that produced the elegant West London garden squares to house the migrants, also accounted for the Gothic-style churches erected at the same time. The churches had not been so much to hallow the squares as to help sell the houses.

The estate churches, paid for by the builders, sanctified by the bishops, and supported by the pew-rents from the affluent new householders, were usually Evangelical, because being Low Church invited no controversy.

In contrast, the so-called private churches were fewer in number and mostly High. They were paid for by people intent to extend their minority brand of churchmanship – a brand often regarded as next to Popery by the others.

'Kengrave Square wasn't built as a square. Not in the first place, Bishop,' provided Tinder. 'The eastern end is quite different from the somewhat dilapidated western end. Moves are afoot to improve things.'

Miss Chorlton smiled to herself. She had known Mr Tinder had a house in Kengrave Square: if there was a posh end it was safe to assume he lived in it. She also knew the square was in the centre of a neighbourhood of mixed accommodation that was being ruthlessly gentrified – where 'somewhat dilapidated' parts would not be tolerated if money could be made out of improving them.

'Remind me where the church is exactly, Lancelot?' said the Bishop.

'At the west end of the square.'

'Yes, I remember now.' The Bishop pulled a face. 'I did go to see it. When I first arrived. But that was two months ago. And you say there's redevelopment going on?'

'A certain amount, yes.' The reply was guarded.

'Could that mean larger congregations eventually?'

'It's possible,' put in the Archdeacon, in a tone suggesting all things were that.

'But unlikely,' countered Tinder. 'One's experience in such matters suggests the opposite.'

'Well, the congregations could hardly get smaller,' complained the Bishop, before changing the subject. 'As I recall, the church isn't remarkable architecturally. Rather the opposite. Redbrick, and looks more like a school. What does the Council for the Care of Churches say? You've got a report from them?'

'It's there with the other documents.' The Archdeacon sighed. 'I'm afraid they don't consider Saint Martin's to be of interest either historically or aesthetically. It's a listed building, of course, but since it's a church, that places no obligation on us to preserve it. And it's not in a conservation area.'

'Do you know the original architect's name?'

'Someone called Henry Conybeare,' supplied the Archdeacon, referring to notes. 'Hardly a name to conjure with, I'm afraid. I believe he'd been a colonial engineer. They say he was advised by the eminent William Bainbridge Reynolds. But perhaps not often enough.' The speaker looked about him with a wan smile.

'So we shan't be accused of vandalism by the Victorian Society? Not if the church is eventually demolished?'

'One would surely look for alternative uses before there was any question of demolition, Bishop?' was the Archdeacon's startled response.

'Such as what alternative use?' demanded Tinder sharply, his chin thrusting at the speaker.

'It could be leased to another denomination,' suggested the Archdeacon.

'The Church Commissioners aren't keen on that any more. Other denominations tend not to honour maintenance agreements,' said the Bishop flatly, scratching his head. 'That was definitely the feeling in my last diocese.'

'Well, if that happened at Saint Martin's the place would fall down in a year,' Tinder put in with great firmness. 'You'll see from the surveyor's report, the roof can't just

14

be patched again. It has to be re-tiled with new bearers. Estimated cost, a hundred and twelve thousand pounds. And that's just the beginning. There's decayed brickwork. The bellcote is bordering on the dangerous. The guttering needs replacing urgently. There's dry rot everywhere, and the electric wiring is actually illegal. I can't see the Coptic Orthodox Church taking that on with a repairing lease.' He leant back with a sharp sniff.

'I meant a religious body of rather more substance than the Coptics,' said the Archdeacon gently, afterwards giving his front teeth a swift, surreptitious press with both thumbs.

'You do mean a Christian body, of course?' Tinder lurched forward again to thirty degrees from the vertical, but back still ramrod straight, and eyes narrowed. 'You weren't thinking of the Muslims or the Hindus?'

The Archdeacon looked confused for two reasons. 'I don't believe I— '

'Alternative uses could also be as a concert hall, a gymnasium, an art gallery,' the Bishop interrupted hastily, it being apparent that the resident of Kengrave Square seated to his left would go down fighting any suggestion of minarets on his doorstep. 'It may even be possible to convert the building into flats or offices.'

'Not offices, I fear, Bishop,' put in Tinder, but not sounding in the least fearful. 'The area is zoned for housing on the Kengrave Square side. With shops at the rear, facing onto Kengrave Road. It might be possible to get a permit for light industrial use on Kengrave Road, but I doubt it.'

Miss Chorlton added a shorthand note for the formal minutes of the meeting: she also construed that Mr Tinder already had a clear idea of what would really happen if St Martin's was demolished.

'Early days yet, in any event,' said the Archdeacon uncheerfully, and before applying his tongue to the needful massaging of his right, upper gum.

'Hardly that, judging by the condition of the fabric.' The Bishop frowned. 'Even if we get draft approval from the Church Commissioners, the diocese still has to maintain the place, until its future's decided. I don't like the sound of that list of dilapidations. How did the church get in such a condition?'

'Quite easily, I'm afraid,' said the Archdeacon. 'Quite a lot has been spent. On essentials. But with such a small congregation, and the building not being in any way famous, raising the wind to pay for major work hasn't been easy. Of course, the same applies to other churches in the diocese. They can't all be of national importance, like Saint Mary Abbots. Or Saint Cuthbert's, Philbeach Gardens.'

'Then all the more reason to press on quickly,' the Bishop responded firmly. 'I gather there'll be no problem with the present incumbent? With the Vicar? You say he's taken another job?'

'A cathedral appointment,' the other clergyman answered, a touch wistfully.

'You've already accepted his resignation, Bishop,' Miss Chorlton prompted in a half-whisper.

'Have I? Good. So if the redundancy goes through, I simply shan't relicense the living. Present chap been there long, has he?'

'Less than two years. He's never been happy,' Tinder volunteered, now more relaxed.

'How does he feel about the church becoming redundant?'

'Resigned.' This was the Archdeacon.

'And he's not opposing in any way?'

'No. His wife—'

'Had some starry-eyed notions about a local campaign to save the place,' Tinder interrupted brusquely. 'After my wife er . . . sensibly abandoned a similar idea. It hasn't come to anything, of course. Anyway, the Vicar will be moving away in a month, taking his wife with him.'

The Bishop nodded. 'And so far as the parish is concerned, you're proposing it be dissolved? Reverting back to the 1874 situation?'

'Yes. The lion's share, including Kengrave Square, will merge into the parish of Saint Winifred's,' said Tinder.

'And the Rural Dean's happy with that?'

'Yes, Bishop,' the Archdeacon replied. 'I spoke to him about it again, earlier this morning.'

'What about Mrs Lodey? The current provider?'

'Keeps very much to herself. Cut above most of the locals,' said Tinder. 'With some exceptions. My wife and I see her from time to time. We're next-door neighbours. She won't know about the redundancy move yet. I'll have a word with her soon. Explain the situation is inevitable. I'm sure she'll understand.'

'Good. There are so few substantial Christian benefactors around nowadays. We mustn't let her go to waste, Lancelot. If you follow me?'

Tinder grinned. 'Have no fear, Bishop. I plan to have her to dine soon with the Vicar of Saint Winifred's. He's good with old ladies.'

'Well just so she doesn't start leading her own campaign to keep Saint Martin's standing.'

'Oh, there's absolutely no fear of that. She's much too decrepit.'

Chapter Two

'And that tiresome Lancelot Tinder had assumed I was far too decrepit to make a fuss, Mr Treasure. I haven't yet chosen entirely to disabuse him of that singular error,' tremoloed the Honourable Mrs Lodey. 'Thank you, Modd,' she added, stabbing a prawn canapé with a cocktail stick – and vehemently so, as if to add portent to her previous remarks.

'But that's quite enough of Mr Tinder for the present,' the old lady continued, glancing from one guest to the other. 'Mrs Treasure, please go on looking at my pictures, if it pleases you. It's such a great satisfaction to have one's things admired by someone so well informed. And your glass needs refilling. Modd, give Mrs Treasure some sherry.'

Each unhurried sentence was delivered with so many modulations and changes in tonal register as to give the impression that the speaker, far from having relinquished merely the desire to control them, actually delighted in their reckless variety. But the diction was clear and resonant. Only an occasional involuntary shake of Mrs Lodey's head hinted at an affliction of advanced age, and if it was that, it was well controlled.

'Just a touch more sherry, Miss Modd. Thank you,' said Molly Treasure with a flash of the famous smile. 'Oh, that's very generous.'

'They're titchy glasses, you know? Hardly one good swallow in 'em,' Miss Modd observed heartily, after pouring nearly to the brim. 'This Amontillado's a drop of the good stuff though, don't you think?' She drew the top of the open decanter close to her nose and took a bosom-heaving deep breath: this seemed to provide the utmost satisfaction.

'Very agreeable, yes,' replied Molly who wasn't wild about sherry, but was managing well enough with this one. 'And this really is such a charming room, Mrs Lodey. The pictures are a feast. Isn't that a Robert Bevan over there?' She moved to examine the painting of a stable yard that was hanging between two long windows at the narrow north end of the oblong, upper-floor drawing room.

'Yes. A distinctive artist and an exciting man. That picture is generally considered to be one of his best. Post-war, of course . . . Nineteen-nineteen,' Mrs Lodey completed when she had remembered the date, not because she had assumed there would be confusion over which war she had meant. She had joined Molly in front of the picture, her movements assisted by an ebony cane with a handsome silver handle.

'There's a Sickert downstairs in the dining room you'll find even more worth coveting, darling,' said Mark Treasure, who had been to the house before. He had remained in the centre of the room with Miss Modd. They were standing before the middle of three windows that offered a view of St Martin's – the church on the opposite side of Kengrave Square.

It was 12.30 on the second Sunday in February, some ten days after the Bishop's meeting with Tinder and the Archdeacon.

Mark Treasure, the merchant banker, and his celebrated actress wife were at Mrs Lodey's for lunch. It was becoming apparent that no one else would be joining them, save for Miss Charmaine Modd, the hostess's companion and housekeeper.

Miss Modd, fiftyish, was a sturdily built, deep-voiced enthusiast with black hair cut short in the masculine manner. She was wearing a tailored tweed coat-and-skirt over a Viyella shirt and knitted tie. That her employer invariably referred to her solely by her surname seemed not to have any demeaning implication: Treasure, at least, understood that Mrs Lodey's companion liked to be addressed in that way by her intimates. Miss Modd was indubitably not a Charmaine, though heaven knew, years ago her mother had tried hard enough to make her one.

'The Camden Town Group were interesting painters. In some ways curiously disparate. Artistically that is.' Mrs Lodey's gaze left the picture, and she began to move back down the room.

'So what brought them together?' asked Molly.

'Good fellowship, and the sound premise that there was commercial sense in numbers. In their selling their pictures as a group. This is nice. A different period, of course,' Mrs Lodey added, in parenthesis, indicating a small wash drawing as she passed it.

'Turner?' questioned Molly who was following.

'We hope so,' the old lady replied with a wan smile, her voice lifting perilously on the 'hope'. 'Of course, I scarcely knew Sickert in the early days. He was older than the others. More celebrated, but with a certain reputation. My mama did not consider him suitable company for an impressionable young girl.' She pronounced the last word as 'gel' in the manner of her upbringing and generation. 'But my father patronised him and many of the others. They broke up as a group before the twenties, of course.' She nodded, this time evidently to affirm the memory, then lowered herself into an upholstered Chippendale armchair to the left of the fireplace, at the south end of the room. 'You'll forgive my sitting?'

Mrs Lodey was eighty-two years old, a shrunken but still striking figure. In her day she had been a noted beauty. She wore her long white hair in a carefully arranged bun which accentuated the slimness of her neck – as did the erect way she held her head and body. The three-quarter-sleeved, calf-length dress she had on had great style. It had been chosen to advantage the delicate wrists as well as the wearer's still pretty ankles – and this despite the season and the outside temperature. Most women were dressed that day in something warmer than silk.

But Mrs Lodey too seldom had the pleasure of a handsome man to luncheon as to allow anything so irrelevant as the weather to govern what she chose to wear.

'Your father was a great collector, Mrs Lodey?' Molly Treasure glanced admiringly at the French gilt clock on the mantelshelf, then settled in a chair across from her hostess. Tall and slim, she was seasonally protected in a lemon wool dress – and glad of it. The temperature in the house was as low as her husband had warned it might be. She wondered how Mrs Lodey survived. There was a fire burning, but one of the fake sort – gas flame around imitation logs. It was generating very little heat. There were radiators, but not many.

'My grandfather, Sir Albert Grenwood, had more taste than my father, though less money with which to indulge it. Nor was my father an antiquarian. He bought pictures and objets d'art by contemporary artists. I inherited a good many things from him. My brother Berty did better, naturally.'

'And your father bought very well,' said Treasure, as he moved across with Miss Modd.

Albert Grenwood had been the joint founder of Grenwood, Phipps, the merchant bankers, where Treasure was Chief Executive. Neither Sir Albert nor his eldest son, the First Viscount Grenwood, had ever been exactly strapped for cash, thanks to the perception of an unennobled forebear who had first backed canals and then got out in time to make a bigger killing in railways. Subsequently, the family fortunes had fluctuated, but the net annual balance had generally moved upwards.

The present Lord Grenwood – Berty, the slightly younger brother of Mrs Lodey – had headed the business well enough until banking had become less a game for gentlemen than a challenge to professionals. At that point he had sensibly eased into the rôle of non-executive chairman, and left the going to Treasure and the high flyers under him. Treasure was still in his early forties.

'It was my grandfather who built this house. That was in 1859. Though it later became too small for him,' Mrs Lodey now offered. 'That was rather before there was a Kengrave Square to speak of. Not that there's much of it in any case. It must be one of the narrowest garden squares in London. And the shortest.'

'From here one can guess fairly easily how it took shape,' said Treasure, turning to look out through the last of the three west-facing windows.

'This house came first at this end. Then the pair of villas next door. They formed the east side,' the hostess continued. 'Later, my grandfather was largely responsible for building the church and vicarage, on spare ground he owned a hundred yards or more to the west. The total cost was a fraction under nine thousand pounds, which seems trivial today, but it was substantial then. What is now the railed garden down the centre of the square was the wide and muddy track the family took to church. Our own garden has always been to the north. Now very attenuated, as you may have noticed.' The graceful head turned to indicate the windows at the other end of the room.

'So the family grassed the muddy track, built pairs of white stucco villas down either side towards the church, and presto, there was a desirable garden square, with all the attributes,' the banker completed.

'Not quite, Mr Treasure. The church was never what could have been termed an estate church. It was put up privately, out of pure piety. My grandfather was a devout Anglo-Catholic. An admirer of Doctor Pusey, the scholar and Tractarian. The new villas were incidental. An after-thought, you might say, though no doubt they were sold for profit.' Mrs Lodey weighed the justice of the point before continuing. 'Unfortunately also, as you will certainly observe, the substantial villas stop some distance before the church. The houses at that end of the square on both sides being of the meaner sort. They were there even before this house was built.'

'Artisans' cottages,' Miss Modd supplied. 'And you can just see there are some even meaner little shops running past the church on both sides. Where the square lets out onto Kengrave Road. It's all rather more Earl's Court than South Kensington.'

'But surely this is the coming area? And artisans' cottages are quite the thing for smartening up. Have been for years,' said Molly. 'In Germoline pink or a biscuit wash, with brightly painted front doors.'

'Not at the other end of Kengrave Square, I'm afraid,' her husband remarked. 'Not yet, anyway.'

'More like a souk along there,' said Miss Modd gruffly. 'Regular eastern market. The terrace houses and the garish shops are in appalling condition. There are a few small restaurants too. Wouldn't catch me feeding in any of 'em, though. But none of it's so appalling as to warrant knocking down by law. Not with the current shortage of houses in London.'

'Who owns them?' asked Treasure.

'A mixture of people.' Miss Modd seemed to be an authority. 'A few are occupied by the freeholders. But most are leasehold. Ends of leases a lot of them, too. With sitting tenants on fixed rents.'

'Is there a developer accumulating the leases?' Treasure asked.

'Yes. D'you know anything about it?' Miss Modd showed keen interest.

'Good lord, no,' the banker answered defensively. 'But looking at it suggests the idea might have occurred to someone.'

'The yards behind the houses are very small. Even the houses at this end,' said Miss Modd, in a still inquisitive tone. 'They back onto a lane. So even if the old houses were cleared, the strips beside the church would be rather narrow for a substantial development, don't you think?'

'For tall blocks of flats, certainly. I had something less ambitious in mind. Short terraces of town houses perhaps.' Treasure turned away from the window. 'In any event, it's the future of the church that's troubling Mrs Lodey.' He thought it time the subject was properly broached: it was what had occasioned the lunch.

The Monday before, Treasure had received an urgent telephone call from Lord Grenwood, who, as usual at this time of year, was enjoying a protracted 'business trip' in sunny Australia. Berty Grenwood had begged Treasure to have a quietening word, as he put it, with his sister, Mrs Lodey. The lady, much incensed, had called her brother in the middle of the previous night, without reference to antipodean time, and Berty was anxious to stop her doing it again. In truth he was frightened of his sister – always had been. She had told him that St Martin's Church was to be made redundant, and demanded to know what he intended to do about it. Berty wouldn't have known what to do about it even if he had been in England. Being eleven thousand miles away he had called Treasure.

Treasure was well acquainted with Mrs Lodey: he was her trustee and, in a less formal way, advised her financially. He certainly wasn't retained to counsel her on the disposition of the churches in her locality, but he had telephoned her about St Martin's shortly after the call from her brother. The result had been the invitation to lunch, accepted because the Treasures were in London for the weekend. It happened Molly and the old lady had never met.

'What did you think of the church, Mrs Treasure?' This was Mrs Lodey.

'Not an architectural gem, and it's obviously seen better days. There are some beautiful altar rails, and a splendidly intricate pulpit. Both in brass and iron. It was horrifyingly cold during the service.'

24

'Many are cold, but few are frozen,' Miss Modd chortled in a near baritone, while settling on the corner of a chaise longue with her knees rather too far apart. 'You should have told us you were going to a service. In Saint Martin's in winter, either you have to keep moving or else double up on your undies.'

'We only decided to go late this morning,' said Treasure. 'Mrs Lodey had mentioned there was an eleven o'clock service.'

'Sung mass,' Miss Modd nodded. 'Well, only sung after a fashion. We go to the eight. We're both early risers, and you don't have to endure a sermon.'

'The sermon was a bit scholarly,' said Treasure.

Molly grimaced. 'Too obscure for me, and very long.'

'The Vicar, Nigel Cudlum, is an academic,' Miss Modd explained, almost in an undertone, as though the man had a socially unacceptable disease. 'Not top flight though. Wouldn't have made it to a professorship anywhere. We think he came here just to do time as a parish priest. To improve his paper qualifications. They say he's been after a cathedral job for years. Well, now he's got one.'

'The altar rails are much remarked, Mrs Treasure,' said the hostess with an approving nod. 'They are quite late Victorian work. Not as old as the church. The pulpit is by the same designer and craftsman. Were there many in the congregation?'

'Six besides us. There seemed to be as many round the altar. Acolytes, I mean. With a rather sweet little Asian boy doing the incense.'

'That's Alan Frakraj. His father's the organist. They're Sri Lankan Christians,' said Miss Modd, a touch dismissively. 'Did you come across Angela Cudlum, the Vicar's wife? Mousey little thing. Mid-thirties. Always in a duffel coat. Got it in a jumble sale two years ago.'

'She spoke to us as we left. Apologised because her husband had had to dash after the service.' This was Molly again. 'She asked if we knew the church was being made redundant. If we were interested in trying to stop that happening.'

'Do you believe I should try to stop it, Mr Treasure?' put in Mrs Lodey suddenly.

'Stopping it would largely be a question of money. I've had some enquiries made. The pressing problem is maintenance. It'll take the thick end of a quarter of a million pounds fully to repair the place. The usual preservation charities don't seem interested in contributing, and the congregation is hardly of a size to find that sort of sum.'

'Ways might be found, even so.' Mrs Lodey touched the side of her mouth with a lace-edged handkerchief.

'Only till the next lot of repairs are due,' said Miss Modd, crossing stout legs and drawing her skirt over her knees. 'It'll be a financial drain for ever. The community's not interested, and the building isn't good enough.'

'One feels a family obligation. My grandfather would have been appalled, quite appalled at the thought of abandoning that church.'

'They say it won't be knocked down. Just fixed up for a different use,' Miss Modd supplied cheerfully.

'There's certainly no guarantee of such an arrangement,' countered the old lady.

'That's true, probably,' said Treasure.

'Wouldn't a new, dynamic vicar change things?' asked Molly.

'Except there's not going to be one,' her husband answered. 'The Bishop isn't going to relicense the living once Cudlum departs. And that's quite soon. What's more the living's in the Bishop's gift.'

'It was originally in the gift of my grandfather. He appointed the first two vicars,' said Mrs Lodey. 'But my father, in his turn, considered that being patron of the living was an inappropriate privilege after he moved to the country. He let it pass to the Bishop. A grave error.'

Treasure took the empty chair at her side. 'To answer your question directly, while the intention does you credit,

I really don't think you should try saving the church single-handed,' he advised with a smile.

'I shouldn't be single-handed,' Mrs Lodey warbled back defiantly, with an enigmatic glance at Miss Modd. 'Perhaps so in the matter of providing funds, but that is only one consideration.'

'But a bloody important one,' countered Miss Modd without dissembling, though quietly enough for her aged employer not to have heard. 'Anyone peckish? Tiffin's ready when you are,' she added loudly.

Chapter Three

'Is Mrs Lodey very rich?' asked Molly, when she and her husband had left Kengrave House after lunch. She linked an arm in his as they set out through the square. They intended taking another look at St Martin's.

'Her family trust fund income is substantial,' Treasure replied. 'For living purposes that is. The capital's entailed, of course.'

'Meaning she can't get her hands on it?'

'That's right. When she dies, her share stays in the pot. To benefit later Grenwoods. Mostly the grandchildren of her two brothers.'

'Whose name is legion. She had no children of her own?'

'One son. Killed in Normandy. In the war. The last war.' Treasure gave a half-smile. 'She's always slightly had it in for her father. Because he left her brothers quite a lot of free capital.'

'But being a girl, he didn't trust her with real money? How disgusting.'

'It was the convention in those days. As it happened, her husband turned out to be a waster, and an alcoholic. If she'd had substantial capital of her own he'd probably have dissipated it for her. He died fairly young. The trust also owns that house and a lot of the contents.'

'Including the pictures?'

'Most of the good ones. The house is leased to her for life at a nominal rent. I've always liked it. Has a lot of style.'

They stopped to glance back at the building. The rendered, snow-white front, under a low, hipped roof, was visible beyond a shoulder-high, stuccoed wall with a wide stone coping. Old iron gates were set into the wall which also protected the garden to the left and beyond, around the corner. The whole property occupied rather more than half the east side of the square.

In relation to its close neighbours, Kengrave House was more rural than urban in character. The other houses were all alike – town villas in mirrored pairs, set behind railings. Each had two storeys and a half-basement, with bay windows rising through all floors. The rather grandiose entrances were served by steps under open porches supported by columns.

'It was a bit warmer in the dining-room,' said Molly as they resumed their walking.

Treasure chuckled. 'It's even warmer out here now.'

The afternoon had become sunny, with a clear blue sky, and two hours left before twilight. The two had come by taxi from their home in Cheyne Walk – not far away on the Chelsea Embankment. They had planned to walk back there.

'I'm surprised she didn't remarry,' said Molly. 'She obviously adored her grandfather. She's pretty fond of you too,' she added, with the practised lift of a perfectly arched eyebrow.

'Well, for once it can't be the older man complex. Berty told me there were several ardent suitors over the years, but she preferred widowhood. Case of once bitten probably.'

'And what about Modd? D'you think she's a . . . ?'

'No. Nothing deviant, if that's what you mean. Just an uncomplicated, hearty spinster.'

'Good cook.'

'Yes. She looks after the old girl very well.'

'But reliable Modd isn't carrying a banner for Saint Martin's.'

'I can guess the reason for that. She's been in the job a good many years. Long enough to expect a legacy to boost her pension. Mrs Lodey has no true dependants. But if she now gives substantial money to the church, when she dies there won't be anything left for deserving employees.'

'But you said she had no capital of her own.'

'No inherited capital. Not to speak of. Not by Grenwood family standards. But she's no spendthrift. Over the years she's consistently saved a bit out of her income, money the bank's invested for her. Her modest portfolio now tots up to about two hundred thousand.'

'Which many would call quite a lot to speak of.' Molly pulled together the collar of her mink coat, in a reflex, if not entirely apposite, show of solidarity with the under-privileged who rubbed along on less than Mrs Lodey's hoard.

'The quality of the housing does tail off at this end,' said Treasure, unmoved by the previous sentiment.

They were approaching the church from the left: the three east windows, tall lancets, disguised the squatness of the brick edifice at this distance. On this side of the church, the road ran westward beside the building to the junction with Kengrave Road, a busy thoroughfare that ran south from Cromwell Road down to Fulham. To the right of the church, and the adjoining vicarage, an alley called Kengrave Place joined the square to the same crossing street.

Most of the shops close to the church were open, despite the day of the week. The Taj Mahal Restaurant was doing late lunch business, most of it in take-away food which some customers were consuming on the pavement outside, across from St Martin's south porch. Eastern music was lamenting from the premises, while similar strains were coming from the less popular Bengal Rôtisserie two doors further on. In between, the Monsoon Laundrette was advertising reduced prices till four o'clock, but with conspicuously few takers observable through its steamy and bannered windows.

'That church roof really looks dicey when you study it closely,' said Treasure, peering upwards.

A mixed-nationality group followed his gaze. They were mostly male Taj Mahal patrons. When none of the participants saw anything to invoke immediate alarm or even interest, they reverted to chewing and studying Molly.

'All very sad,' said the actress, about the roof, as the two crossed over the road and entered the projecting porch. 'You know, a Gothic church without a tower or steeple somehow never looks complete. The bellcote makes the place look more like a school.' She peeped out to the right, through an opening in the porch, and down into the narrow basement area, spanned by the porch. The gap between the church wall and the pavement was railed. A gate in the railings opened onto a stone stairway, also railed. The steps ran down to a door into the basement, directly under the main porch. 'That must be the door to the crypt,' Molly concluded, poking her head out further.

'Church hall, I think.'

'Listen. Is there music coming from down there?'

'Don't think so. It's from across the road.' Treasure was examining the notice board. 'Quite a lot goes on in the church hall, though. Including a protest meeting on Thursday evening about the closing of the church.' He pointed to a neat, hand-drawn notice. 'That wasn't there this morning.'

'This one was.' Molly was now scanning a closely printed, official looking announcement with typed additions. 'It's about the Church Commissioners declaring Saint Martin's redundant. Says anybody opposed should lodge their objection before April the first.'

'At least it's a church that stays open all Sunday, despite the vandal problem,' said Treasure, now holding the heavy door ajar for his wife.

'Just like the Bengal Rôtisserie opposite,' Molly replied brightly. 'They're not doing much trade either. There's evensong here at six. Perhaps we should stay on for compline and curry?'

Inside, the church gave the appearance of great width because it was single span with no structural divisions for the side aisles. The chancel arch was pointed, with lower arches on either side both blocked – the one on the left by organ pipes rising behind a side altar, and the other by a wooden vestry screen. The natural light was poor since there was no clerestory. The only functional high windows were the three slim ones at the west end. Even so, a single shaft of sunlight was streaking through dramatically from one of these to the sanctuary, making parts of the gilt-encrusted reredos shimmer. It was this ornate reredos, free-standing, but reaching to the roof, that excluded light from the east windows behind it. There was a narrow processional way around the altar and reredos, beyond the lateral sections of the altar rails that boxed in the sanctuary on three sides.

In the nave, there were two rows of ten pews separated by a wide aisle. Marks elsewhere on the wooden floor witnessed that there had formerly been many more pews behind these, in the main body of the church, as well as in the side aisles. The surviving pews looked marooned – more so than they had done to the Treasures on the earlier visit when the couple had come in as the service was starting.

Now there were no candles burning, no one moving around the altar, no sound of any kind except the noise of the visitors' own footfalls as they approached the chancel.

To the right, near the vestry door, were the forlorn remnants of a dismantled Christmas crib. Not far from those, an isolated trestle table against a peeling wall bore the equally abandoned remnants of a poster and leaflet appeal for starving Ethiopians.

Apart from the tract case near the door, there was only the reservation lamp burning in front of the side altar and the lingering pall of incense to witness the church was in active use at all.

And then, as though to confound the impression of desertion, suddenly someone began to play a triumphant and instantly familiar strain on the organ – a staccato, four-chord repeat, followed by another similar bar, but with the fourth chord ascending. The musical pattern was followed with increasing volume right up the scale until the main melody of Mendelssohn's 'Wedding March' came crashing through the air – and Molly's spontaneous peal of laughter.

'Perhaps we don't look married enough already,' she cried delightedly, both hands clasping her husband's arm.

It happened the two had just reached the sanctuary steps and had been standing there side by side.

Then the music stopped in mid-bar, as suddenly as it had begun. There was the sound of a metal-ringed curtain being thrust back, and of feet descending heavily on wood.

'I am most dreadfully sorry. I have disturbed you?' The dark-skinned organist was hurrying forward into the chancel from behind the choir stalls on the left. His face was suffused with concern.

'Not at all. I wish you'd go on playing. Mr Frakraj isn't it?' said Treasure, who was good at remembering names.

'Sundar Frakraj, at your service, sir. And who have I the honour of addressing?' The speaker was beaming now, something that better fitted the good-humour lines sunk into the skin around eyes and mouth than the worried frown had done earlier. He was middle aged, and a touch overweight, with a nose that flared as he breathed, and bushy eyebrows that moved a good deal when he spoke. There was not a lot of hair left on the top of his head, though what remained was shiny black, not grey. He wore heavily framed spectacles, and was casually but neatly dressed in a red, roll-necked sweater and grey flannels. His words had been mannerly not obsequious.

Treasure introduced himself and his wife, adding: 'We were at the eleven o'clock service.'

'Oh, my goodness me.' Hands were lifted in despair. 'You've suffered Frakraj's musical desecrations enough for one day.'

'Not at all. You play beautifully,' said Molly.

'I'm thinking not so well as you act, Mrs Treasure. You are the celebrated Miss Molly Forbes, I'm sure. Many times I've seen you on the television. Also once on the stage. In a play by Sir Arthur Pinero. You were very good. Sadly, I don't have the time to go often to the theatre. If I did, it would be to see you.'

'How gallant you are, Mr Frakraj,' said Molly. 'Tell me, do you have a lot of weddings here?'

The organist sighed. 'None at all. But we live in hopes. I practise the "Wedding March", as the French say, to encourage the others.'

'We came back to look at the artefacts in the church. Especially the metalwork.' Treasure indicated the altar rails.

'Very handsome. Very refined,' said the organist. 'Believed to be the work of Ernest Geldart. Also the pulpit, which is more Spanish than English, don't you think? The reredos behind the altar, that's not so pleasing. Too gaudy. It's much earlier work. Artist unknown.'

'You know your church well,' Molly complimented.

'There are not too many remarkable things in it, Mrs Treasure. If there were, probably we shouldn't be facing redundancy. You know about that?'

'Mrs Lodey's been telling us. We've just had lunch with her.'

'Ah, Mrs Lodey. Now there is a lady. Of the old school. A pleasure to serve. She comes to my store still. From time to time. For our special blend of tea.'

'Which is your store, Mr Frakraj?' Molly asked. 'I must come there myself.'

Frakraj looked pleased, the eyes blinking frequently behind the glasses. 'Actually, I have two stores. A country one. In Cordley. That's near Epsom in Surrey.'

'We know the village. It's very pretty. But too far for me to shop,' Molly observed with a grin.

'The other store is not in such a genteel area, I'm afraid. In Kengrave Road. Next to the church. On the other side to the main porch, where you came in. It's called the Full Moon Supermarket. Silly name, but it helps people to remember we're open at night. Quite late. On Sundays as well. But Sunday in the morning and evening only. Not the afternoon.'

'Shall you be joining the protest about the church?'

The speaker's face showed a momentary embarrassment. 'To support Mrs Cudlum? We shall all do that. But I'm thinking it will take much money and influence to achieve something. To change the Bishop's plan.'

'Then you think closure will come?' This was Treasure. 'Certainly the church seems poorly attended.'

Frakraj's beam had returned. 'This part is not well attended. You must come to see the other. Please? Come now, won't you?'

With great determination, the organist had turned on his heel and set off past the choir stalls and the organ. Then, with one beckoning hand in the air, he hurried along a short passage which ended in three doors – one facing and one on either side.

'Door into the vicarage,' said Frakraj, halting and pointing to the one ahead. 'On the right the door to the sacristy. And this one takes us down to the church hall. It's unlocked.' He turned the iron ring-latch. 'Please to take extra care on the steps, Mrs Treasure.'

The narrow linoed stairs were enclosed in wood, and turned at a landing in the middle. A door at the bottom stood open.

'It's very noisy,' was Molly's first exclamation.

'Because it's very well attended,' Frakraj replied, nodding with pleasure.

It was the extreme warmth and bright light that first struck the visitors, compared to the place they had just left.

The basement was low-ceilinged and large, if not quite as large as the church above. Certainly it was big enough comfortably to accommodate at the near end a dozen old ladies playing whist at three tables, a group of youths dismembering two old sofas under the direction of an aristocratic young man, and after that, four youngsters engaged in a vigorous and rowdy game of table tennis. And these were only the activists who first came into sight. Further along there was a full-size billiard table, also in use. Then came a dozen children of various ages and skin colours kneeling on cushions, and blowing furiously on small wind instruments. These were being instructed by a cheerful-looking girl in her late teens.

The Treasures took in the scene as they followed their guide down the centre of the room. He was leading them to a long trestle table at the end which bore a stack of cups, saucers and plates, and an inviting selection of what it pleased Treasure to note were home-made cakes. Behind the table, to one side against the wall, was a cooker and a chromium tea-urn set over a gas-burner.

Mrs Cudlum, and another woman – younger and much more attractive – were filling the urn with water from jugs as the newcomers approached. The Vicar's wife waved the urn top at Molly before jamming it back in place. 'Glad to see you again so soon,' she called with a smile, and seeming a lot more confident than she had been at their first encounter. 'Tea'll be ready shortly.'

'Thanks, but we've only just finished lunch,' said Molly. 'We're here because Mr Frakraj wanted to impress us with the activity.'

'And we're duly impressed,' Treasure added. 'Are the cakes available on a take-away basis, perhaps?'

'Not usually, but we can always make an exception,' said Mrs Cudlum. 'This is the Sunday Club. We don't have rigid rules. Bit of a hodgepodge, but the club serves a lot of purposes. This is Miss Garely. Kate Garely. Does the refreshments with me, makes the cakes, and runs a free aerobics class here in the week as well. She's really the director of physical education at the Comprehensive up the road.' She put a hand around the other's shoulder. 'We couldn't do without Kate.'

Miss Garely looked to be in her late twenties. 'But you're Molly Forbes. We're honoured,' she offered brightly. 'Mrs Cudlum said you were at the eleven o'clock service. I missed it for once, so it's marvellous to meet you after all.' She had almond-shaped brown eyes, high cheekbones, a generous mouth, and a slim, athletic figure. Her honey-coloured hair was swept back tightly from her tanned forehead and tied in a pony-tail. Before she had finished speaking she had moved the interested gaze from Molly to her escort.

'My name's Mark Treasure. Molly Forbes' husband,' he said with a grin.

'With a penchant for home-baked cakes?' The young woman grinned back, wide-eyed.

'I beg your pardon. I should have introduced everybody properly.' This was Frakraj, confused.

'Tell us what they're doing with those sofas?' asked Treasure, while shaking hands with Kate Garely.

'Making them like new.' It was Mrs Cudlum who replied with enthusiasm, and in an accent the banker had already placed as a lot closer to Birmingham than to Sloane Square.

'They're the kind that open into beds,' Miss Garely added. 'Perfect for old people who can only afford to heat one room in winter. We get a lot of broken-down ones from a local auctioneer. For nothing, of course. We fix them up, then give them to people in need.'

'Is the young man in charge really a carpenter?' Molly enquired. 'He looks more like a guards' officer.'

'That's Peter Windle. He's an accountant,' said Mrs Cudlum. 'He can do anything with his hands though. And the leader of the recorder band is Caroline Tinder. She's a full-time music student. Her mother's churchwarden at Saint Martin's. The helpers all give time on Sundays. In relays. It's the day a lot of welfare clubs are closed.' The speaker was evidently proud of her volunteers.

'What will happen to the Sunday Club if the church is shut?' asked Molly.

'Oh, we're not dependent on the church,' was the surprising reply from the Vicar's wife. 'Hardly any of our customers are churchgoers. Quite a few are Hindu or Muslim. Isn't that right, Sundar?'

'Quite right,' answered Frakraj solemnly. 'But I'm thinking there's always the possibility of conversions,' he concluded, though the words sounded more speculative than hopeful.

'Whatever happens upstairs, we intend to carry on as usual down here,' Mrs Cudlum completed.

'That could be wishful thinking when you've left, of course,' put in Kate Garely.

'Without Mrs Cudlum everything will close,' said Caroline Tinder who had just joined the group at the refreshment table. 'Can I have the Cokes for my thirsty lot, please? And they're all dying to ask for your autograph, Miss Forbes.' She was a jolly girl, quite pretty and fairly buxom, with a peaches-and-cream complexion.

'I'll give autographs in return for a spirited rendering of "Greensleeves" by the recorder orchestra,' said Molly. 'It's what you were practising when we came in.'

'Done,' said the girl. 'If you can stand the racket. I'm afraid the recorder isn't all that melodious. But it's the easiest of the wind instruments to learn.'

'Except for the tin whistle,' offered Treasure. 'But I

suppose that's not a real instrument. What are you studying at college, Caroline?'

'Not the recorder,' she answered with an embarrassed grin. 'Piano and flute actually.'

'She's a very promising pianist,' said Frakraj earnestly.

'Are you joining the campaign to keep the church open?' The girl had addressed her question to Molly. 'We'll need a leader when Mrs Cudlum's gone. It'd be marvellous to have a celebrity.'

'Not really my scene, I'm afraid. Also, shouldn't it be someone from the parish?'

'Suppose so.' This was Caroline again. 'My mother's given up, I'm afraid. And Daddy says it's a hopeless cause anyway. He thinks they'll have to pull the church down within a year.'

'It'll be over my dead body if they do,' announced Mrs Cudlum – impetuously, judging from her blushes afterwards.

Chapter Four

'It wasn't so long ago that having the Russian Ambassador as speaker at an American function would have been unthinkable,' said Treasure.

It was an early afternoon on the Wednesday following the visit to Kengrave Square.

'As unthinkable as having the Russian Ambassador admit that he even spoke English,' agreed Sir James (Jumbo) Crib-Cranton, also seated in the back of Treasure's Rolls-Royce. 'They all did speak English, I'll bet.'

'This chap today made quite a lot of sense, I thought.'

'Now and again,' the other allowed, but grudgingly: he took a cold-war view of Russia still. 'This traffic's appalling. Let me out opposite Fortnum's, Henry, will you? That's if we ever get there. No need to go down to the square. Might have been quicker to walk.'

'Very good, Sir James,' answered Henry Pink, Treasure's chauffeur, who agreed with the last comment. They had scarcely progressed at all down Park Lane in the several minutes since leaving the Grosvenor House Hotel. The two passengers had been guests there at an American Chamber of Commerce lunch.

'Anyway, the company was good, Mark. You know more about Russo–American relations than I do, of course. Good of Marvin what's-his-name to invite us and will you just look at that girl's legs? My word,' the speaker had changed the subject without punctuation or change of breath, but with a sharply accelerated delivery.

Sir James, known universally as Jumbo since his international rugby-playing days, was chairman of CCB, one of Britain's largest construction companies, and a major corporate client of Grenwood, Phipps. He was also, at fifty-nine, a practised – you could almost say learned – judge of the female form. His senatorial head had turned to follow the progress of the long-limbed beauty he'd spotted on the pavement. He was glaring through the rear window as he added: 'Wonder what makes them bother wearing skirts at all when they get that short?'

'The law, I expect,' said Treasure drily, prepared for more comment on manifestations of transitory Mayfair wildlife while traffic movement was slow, and until a subject of more interest to Jumbo evolved – except there weren't many of those, not after lunch. 'How's Ariadne?' the banker enquired as a levelling shot. Ariadne was Jumbo's wife – his fourth wife. In a paradoxical way she was proof of her husband's often repeated contention that he was no irresponsible philanderer – a view that in logic even his detractors found it difficult to refute.

'Ariadne's in fine condition, thank you,' Jumbo replied, a trifle absently, as though they were discussing one of the expensive fillies in his Berkshire stable. He settled his formidable frame back into the seat. His facial expression offered no suggestion that Treasure's enquiry had exercised the sobering effect intended. This might have been because the twenty-eight-year-old Ariadne was currently very pregnant – more incontestable evidence of Jumbo's unfrivolous intentions.

'That reminds me, Mark. Know anything about a property group called Aziz Developments? Head man's Turkish.'

Treasure just followed the tenuous connection. Ariadne's mother, he recalled, had been Greek. 'Never heard of them,' he replied. 'Should I have done?'

'Yes, you should,' said Jumbo with satisfaction. That and the glint behind the half-spectacles implied that what he classified as serious 'bird watching' was no more deserving of admonition than was a careless attitude to market intelligence. 'The Aziz people bandy your name about freely enough.' With a great heave, he produced a handkerchief from a side pocket of the blue pin-stripe jacket.

'My name or the bank's?'

Jumbo blew his large nose loudly. 'The bank's, but it's all the same,' he added, aware that it wasn't at all the same, but not wanting to spoil his earlier point. 'They've got two quite interesting developments on the go. We're bidding on both. One's an office complex in Peterborough. The other's in West London. Smaller. A block of flats with shops underneath, plus a few houses. Top quality stuff though.'

'And I assume Grenwood, Phipps is supposed to be staking Aziz Developments?'

'That's what Akro Aziz told me. He's the chairman.'

'When are the start dates?'

'The Peterborough job's early next year. The other one depends on planning permission still. The plans and specifications are finished on both.'

'Even so, any funding through us won't need to have been ratified yet. So it's not surprising I haven't come across it,' Treasure concluded easily. 'Big money involved?'

'The building costs in Peterborough won't offer much change out of twenty-five million. I don't know what they're paying for the land. The West London job'll be a lot less than that. Say ten million for construction. Depends a bit on whether the local authority allows an extra storey on the main building. The flats.'

Treasure watched the traffic lights at Hyde Park Corner, willing them not to change from green to yellow before Henry Pink had turned the big car left onto Piccadilly. 'What part of West London?' he asked, as the car surged through the intersection.

'Kengrave Square. Backing onto Kengrave Road. It's one of the coming areas.'

'There's a church at that end of Kengrave Square.'

'Is there? Well I doubt it'll be there much longer.'

Jumbo dismissed what seemed to him to be a self-evident truth: he was not himself a great churchgoer, except for Christmas and memorial services. 'The thing is, are Aziz Developments good for that kind of lolly? We've never dealt with them before.'

'Presumably your people have cleared with us that the projects are funded? That's if we're committed.'

'We've got that from down the line, certainly,' Jumbo answered blankly. 'Rather hear it from the horse's mouth though. Fact is, we need that sort of business these days. But it's easy to get carried away.'

'I'll check, and call you this afternoon.'

Treasure suspected his involvement would be superfluous. It wasn't even that thirty-five million pounds was a large sum in relation to the total value of the contracts CCB normally handled. He was sure, too, that his companion was dramatising when he implied his company needed contracts so badly that they took undue risks over credit. It was more likely that the Chairman of CCB wanted it known to his subordinates that he and the Chief Executive of the bank had exchanged a private word on the Aziz matter – as an example of Jumbo's lively and responsible interest. Such ploys were not uncommon even with top industrialists – even ones who scarcely needed to court approbation for its own sake. But then Jumbo did have immature aspects to his nature.

That was Treasure's immediate view, though it was to be revised later. He would ordinarily have been content to indulge the other's whim: in truth, because of the Kengrave Square involvement, he could scarcely wait to do so.

'Stop, Henry. This'll do. Right here. Thanks again for the lift, Mark. You won't forget the other matter? Talk to you later.' Jumbo was halfway out of the car before it had properly stopped. He would scarcely have moved more quickly if the vehicle had been on fire. Once on the pavement, he stuck his head back in. 'What about that one then?' he challenged with guttural enthusiasm, and as a final shot before he closed the door and strode off in the wake of a tall brunette in very tight jeans, the evident cause of his electric leavetaking. Jumbo was bird watching again – the cause of his having alighted a block before he had intended, and that much further from his own office in St James's Square, in spite of the cold and his having no overcoat.

'Ah Gerald, just the man. Got a minute before the meeting?' asked Treasure, as he got out of the lift on his return to the Grenwood, Phipps building in the City.

'Sure. Ten minutes, if you want.'

Gerald Head, one of the joint managing directors of the bank, was short, and thick-set, with a rolling walk. He was the same age as Treasure who he now followed from the carpeted corridor into the other's office on the third floor.

'There are notes about two calls on your desk, Mr Treasure,' said Miss Gaunt, Treasure's mature and imperturbable secretary, as the two men passed her desk. 'And Mr Pugh would like to see you after the review meeting which he can't attend. It's about the privatisation flotation. Shall I give him a time? You could do four-thirty.' She had notebook and pencil poised.

'It's urgent?'

Miss Gaunt blinked in a manner that just might have implied that she wouldn't have bothered asking if it hadn't been. 'He has to see the Minister again in the morning,' she announced dourly, as though that might be the last anyone would ever see of Mr Pugh.

Treasure glanced at his watch. 'Four-thirty's fine.'

Miss Gaunt's long, intelligent face relaxed as she reached for the internal telephone.

A moment later, Treasure waved Head toward a chair at the circular meeting table in his office. 'I've been trying to remember if you're reporting on an outfit called Aziz Developments today?' He flipped through the top pages of a folder he'd picked up from his desk before joining the other at the table.

Both men were due shortly at the bank's fortnightly top management review meeting. This was where projected major new activities were outlined, and less important ones tabled for information. It was usually not a long meeting, and was primarily intended as an exercise in quick communications. The folder in Treasure's hand contained the agenda and supporting papers.

'No. You won't find Aziz on my list. They're jibbing at the modest rates of interest we're proposing.' Head's countenance was rounded and flat – and some said inscrutable. This was witness to his partly oriental origins. But at the moment he was registering mild amusement. 'Has Jumbo Crib-Cranton been onto you by any chance?'

'We just sat next to each other at the American lunch.'

'That explains it. I wondered how you'd come on Aziz otherwise. It's fairly small beer as yet. Well run, though. Akro Aziz, the chairman, is a sound entrepreneur. Plenty of flair, and knows his business. The company could go far.'

'And also go public?'

'Very probably. Assets are well employed. Loan capital demands reasonable. They've outgrown the clearing bank they've been with. That's why they came to us. Problem is, they don't like our rates. Or pretend they don't. They'll come round.'

Gerald Head was in charge of the conventional banking division at Grenwood, Phipps. This involved lending money, short- or long-term, or arranging credits or guarantees with the bank as backer. The customers might be private individuals, companies of all sizes, and occasionally even governments. This is not as glamorous a merchant-banking activity as, say, corporate finance which deals in takeovers and flotations. Nor is it as frenzied as the work of the treasury division that trades in foreign exchange, nor as intellectually demanding as the investment department which looks after massive pension funds. But when it comes to profit making, no other activity contributes as much to the merchant-banking pot so consistently as the old-fashioned, bedrock function of lending money at interest.

'I gather CCB are after two of the Aziz building contracts,' said Treasure.

'And lining up for a third much bigger one. Didn't Jumbo tell you that?'

'No. He suggested CCB would be on the breadline if they didn't get these other two. Which was obviously nonsense.' Treasure's eyes narrowed. 'So the real angle is to get a third project by doing a good job on the others? Very big is it?'

'Medium. Two-fifty million, including land costs. For a new shopping centre near the M25 motorway. We'd quite like to be in on that too.'

'But not to the extent of cutting our margins for Aziz now?'

'No. And we shouldn't have to. What we've offered is competitive.' Head's mouth gave an enigmatic wince. 'On the whole, I'd say Jumbo intended you should direct our thinking to be easier on Aziz Developments.'

'And will have told Mr Aziz as much.' Treasure nodded. 'That'll be it, of course. Devious devil. Naturally he knew any checking by me would bring out the interest rate problem. All he actually asked me to do was get a view on the Aziz creditworthiness.'

'Oh, that's impeccable. To date anyway.'

'Then I'll tell him just that. That'll fox him.'

In an energetic movement, Head folded his short arms across his barrel chest. 'D'you want me to have our loan agreements on Aziz reworked? To see if we can cut anywhere? I don't believe we'll find any slack.' He paused. 'CCB are important customers, after all.'

'Certainly not, Gerald. Not for that reason.' Treasure knew better than to convert unintended intervention into actual interference.

'We'll have a look anyway,' said Head with a grin, which was what Treasure had wanted him to say.

'You must please yourself about that. Incidentally, I have a remote personal interest in the second Aziz project. The Kengrave Square development. You won't know the detail of that.'

'Yes I do. Thirty, or potentially, thirty-six flats in one block with a basement carpark, and flanked by twenty-four town houses in two terraces of twelve. The whole scheme is still waiting on various formal consents. The extra six flats depends on whether Aziz gets approval for a sixth floor to the building. They've done the basic costing on building five floors.'

'But an extra floor on the same bit of land would make a big difference to the end profit?'

'A spectacular difference. It'd just about double it.'

As always, Treasure was impressed by the other's capacity for instant, detailed recall on a project that had to be one of hundreds he was currently dealing with, a good many larger than this one.

'You know there's a church on the site at the moment?' Treasure asked.

'Mm. And some decayed shops and houses. Aziz has been quietly collecting leases on those for years.'

'The church is still operational.'

'One of the reasons the whole development is still on ice. It should be moving within a year though.'

'With the church demolished?'

Head shrugged. 'Before it falls down, apparently. The Church of England doesn't want it any more. It's of no architectural merit. And the cost of converting it into flats would be greater than starting again.'

'Seems to me a good deal's been taken for granted, even so.'

'Not really. The church is certainly going to be made redundant. Aziz has made it known in the right quarters what he'll give for the site, including demolishing what's

47

on it. That's the way to please the Church Commissioners. Offer them money and save them trouble. Can't blame them for that. The local authority likes the look of the Aziz development plan. Remember, it replaces a church that pays no local taxes with a bunch of new residents who will.'

'But my point is that none of this can have been formally approved by anyone,' Treasure put in uneasily.

'Ah, now I see what you mean. About it being taken for granted. In the formal sense that's true. But most property projects are fixed up informally in advance these days. Behind the scenes, as it were. Saves time in the end. Oh, nothing sinister about that,' he responded to Treasure's raised eyebrows. 'Intelligent anticipation means that funds are lined up ready for the off. For when formal approvals are issued. The other way round, if the money isn't immediately available, everybody suffers frustration and delay till it is.'

Treasure still looked unconvinced. He glanced at the time. 'Suppose we'd better go into the meeting. Tell me, Gerald, have you ever met the Honourable Mrs Lodey?'

'You mean Berty's sister? No I haven't. Why?'

Both men moved towards the door. 'I just wondered. She lives in Kengrave Square. Their grandfather built that church. I wouldn't absolutely count on it being knocked down. Not just yet.'

Chapter Five

'His name's Smurt. Marvin Smurt,' said Miss Gaunt. 'He said he'd wait on the off chance of your seeing him. I said it was very unlikely . . . but possible.' She had hesitated before the last two words. 'It was only that he'd come from Mrs Lodey. That's why I went down. He says it's about a confidential matter. It was rather difficult, Mr Treasure.'

Miss Gaunt did not normally admit difficulty. On the contrary, difficulty was precisely what she was known for overcoming.

'And he's still downstairs. What's he like?' Treasure studied the visiting card Miss Gaunt had handed him.

It was four-forty. The review meeting had ended, but it had overrun. Treasure had expected to find an impatient Ewan Pugh, Head of Corporate Finance, waiting for him in his office. But Pugh had been summoned very urgently to Whitehall to see the Minister for the Environment, in place of the arrangement to see him next day. Treasure hoped this meant the Government's latest privatisation plan was off again, temporarily excusing Grenwood, Phipps, and other bankers in a consortium, from underwriting what the City was viewing as an untimely flotation. It also meant he had the time to see Marvin Smurt if he chose.

'He's very tall, even for an American,' Miss Gaunt replied. 'Quite young. Early forties, I should say.' The speaker was forty-seven. 'He's in London for ten days.'

That she had volunteered nothing about the character of Smurt was a credit to Miss Gaunt's objectivity, or so her employer construed. The card described the caller as

International Executive Vice-President of the Community of Investors for Jesus Incorporated – an organisation which, on the face of it, was unlikely to commend itself to a conservative, straight-down-the-middle Roman Catholic like Emily Gaunt.

'I see.' He was thinking of Mrs Lodey, and his near-pledge to Berty Grenwood not to give her new grounds for telephoning Australia in the middle of the night. 'I'd better see him. Break in after ten minutes will you?'

'Yes, Mr Treasure.' Miss Gaunt nodded approvingly.

It had been a tactful compromise. For Treasure to have turned the visitor away would have put in question his secretary's decision to offer hope of an audience without appointment: on the other hand, to see him for ten minutes did nothing to undermine her religious scruples – nor to commend Mr Smurt's.

'Mighty good of you to see me, Mr Treasure. Yes-sir.'

Smurt seemed to lower the ceiling height when he entered Treasure's office. He was not merely tall, he towered. The handshake was if anything over-firm, except the banker's attention was absorbed at the time by the man's stature and then by the slightly absurd black walrus moustache that enveloped his upper lip – so prominent that it seemed to overbalance the wearer.

'Do sit down. What can I do for you?'

Smurt took one of the leather armchairs in front of Treasure's desk. He leant forward with a shy expression, holding a document case on his lap. He drew a hand through his thick but short-cut hair. 'Kengrave House advised you might look after a deposit of money for Jesus.' The voice that filtered through the moustache was soft, and as tentative as the statement.

'We're a merchant bank, yes. We invest funds for clients. Substantial funds.' Treasure gave a tolerant smile. It amused him to be styled as God's potential banker, as well as to have the two residents of Kengrave House made to sound like a financial advice group. Even so, he had more important things to do than act as teller for church collections. 'I think you might find one of the clearing banks more convenient for your purposes. For instance, Lloyds or Barclays would—'

'Oh, we have a chequeing account over here already. And the deposit I mentioned is substantial. Quite substantial.' Smurt looked over his shoulder, while pawing at the neck of the buttoned-down shirt. He turned back again to Treasure, swallowed, then added: 'Yes-sir. It's like fifty million dollars?' There was a crack as he suddenly brought his teeth together, loudly and savagely, in the lantern jaw. 'That's to start an accumulator fund for the UK. We shouldn't need to use more than half of it on setting up costs. But we'd add to it again in due time. That's confidential, you understand?'

'Naturally.' The banker had been as much unnerved by the savage snapping of the teeth as surprised at the size of the sum. 'What exactly are you setting up?'

'A channel of spiritual and human communication over here, Mr Treasure. A European extension of the Community of Investors for—'

'I see,' the banker interrupted. 'Would this be a religious community? Like a monastery perhaps?'

'For heaven sakes, no, Mr Treasure. I guess you'd think of us as television evangelists. But there's a difference. We have a regular cable congregation of half a million back home. Now that's not big by American standards. But the quality of our following is unique. That's the difference. Our leader, Brother Jethro, he wants to start the good work here just as soon as possible.'

'Ah. There you'll have problems, I imagine. That kind of religious broadcasting isn't er . . . isn't practised in this country. Under the laws covering television—'

'We know all about that, Mr Treasure, sir. At the start we'll just be making recordings in Britain. Transmission will be by American-owned satellite. That's till things change over here.'

'You're expecting changes?'

'Oh, sure. No question.' Smurt looked over his shoulder again sharply before continuing. 'Meantime, the CIJ TV studio.' He paused. 'CIJ standing for the Community of Investors for Jesus?' He waited for Treasure's nod of comprehension before continuing. 'It needs to be operational by summer. We have a place picked out.'

After the head turning, Treasure had steeled himself for another compulsive crack of the teeth, but none came. 'Is that somewhere offshore perhaps?' he enquired.

'Nothing like that, Mr Treasure. We're not pirates. We're humble apostles of the Lord. We aim to buy the church in Kengrave Square. It's perfect for what we need. Right size and location. For recording services and seminars.'

But presumably the Community of Investors for Jesus television studio was not expected to operate from one of Mr Aziz's flats. 'Have you started negotiating with anyone for the church?'

'Not yet, sir. That's where we need more advice.'

It seemed the Investors for Jesus weren't the only ones. 'Did Mrs Lodey offer any?'

'We didn't meet with Mrs Lodey. No-sir.' Now the teeth came together again, between sentences – like a dog snapping at a fly – and taking Treasure off guard. 'It was Miss Modd we saw. That's Mrs Lodey's business manager?'

Treasure had reservations about the description, but he let them pass. He was resolving to check later whether Smurt had admitted to Miss Gaunt that he hadn't seen Mrs Lodey herself. 'Might I ask why you went to Kengrave House in the first place?'

'Surely. There was no one home in the vicarage, and a lady in the church hall, that's in the basement, she said to try there.'

'If you wanted to buy the church?'

'For information on when the church was becoming redundant,' Smurt corrected. 'Miss Modd was very helpful.

She told me that in the regular way, Saint Martin's wouldn't be up for sale for some while. But with the roof coming apart and all, something would need to be done soon.'

'I think that's possibly true. She didn't suggest you see the Bishop or the Archdeacon?'

'Well now.' Smurt checked over his shoulder. 'The fact is, Mr Treasure, she did suggest something of that kind. And I had to explain that while the Investors for Jesus welcomes people of all Christian persuasions, and many who have had no persuasion at all, we don't always find our attitude reciprocated. Especially by leaders of the traditional churches.' He combed the moustache gravely with all four fingers of one hand. 'It varies, of course.'

'But probably not to the extent of such people being prepared to sell you their left-over churches?' Treasure nodded. 'But you'd tried to see the Vicar in the first place?'

'Those in the humbler offices are often more understanding than the high-ups. We have many of them come over to work as territory counsellors to our congregation.'

'Converts?'

'Men and women who've given up being losers as ministers of failing communions. Who've opted to be Investors for Jesus.'

'I see. So Miss Modd suggested you came to me?'

The other nodded enthusiastically. 'She said you'd know how we should go forward, and how to look after our funds.'

It was difficult to decide for whom Miss Modd had thought she was doing the favour. 'I noticed from your card that your organisation is incorporated. It's a private company, I assume?'

'Yes-sir. You'd like a copy of our last balance sheet and accounts?' Smurt snapped open the document case.

'That would be useful.' The banker had been pleased by the visitor's anticipation. He accepted the slim document, and gave the appearance of casually flipping through its pages while applying a practised eye to absorbing the key contents.

'Naturally, we'd look to you for advice about whether we need to form a subsidiary company over here, Mr Treasure.'

The banker looked up at the speaker's face for a moment before deciding what to say next. 'I appreciate you're on a tight schedule, Mr Smurt, but can you leave the whole matter with me until, shall we say, Friday morning?'

'Be glad to, sir. You'll find we check out all right. I have a list of corporate referees here.' He withdrew another sheet from his case and passed it over.

'Thank you. It's not simply a matter of checking out your organisation, though I admit we should like to do that. We should need also to be sure there was no conflict of interest between yourselves and other customers. That's in your own interest, as well as ours.'

'I understand, Mr Treasure. Or I think I do. You mean Grenwod, Phipps have other religious organisations—'

'No. Nothing like that.' Treasure was not prepared to disclose that the bank could hardly be party to an Investors for Jesus attempt to take over St Martin's church if it was funding Aziz Developments to do the same thing.

In normal circumstances, the unfortunate coincidence of the Aziz intention could have been enough to make Smurt's business unacceptable, at least for the time being. Also, from what he knew of American television evangelists, the banker considered Grenwood, Phipps should probably steer clear of taking one as a customer in any case, for a number of hard-nosed reasons.

By choosing to keep the matter alive for a little, Treasure was principally motivated by the same private interest he had admitted to Gerald Head earlier – a sense of personal obligation to Mrs Lodey. Also, he had to admit he had been impressed by the first cursory glance at the accounts still in his hand.

'If we're not able to accept your business, I doubt

the delay will be entirely wasted,' Treasure continued. The most likely event, he thought, would be his having to advise Smurt not to pursue the idea of buying St Martin's against determined and already entrenched competition. He pushed his chair away from the desk in obvious preparation for concluding the meeting. 'So, if we might leave it there?'

'So why do they want Saint Martin's so badly,' asked Molly Treasure later that day. 'I mean, I can understand the development company wanting it. But these Attestors for Jesus—'

'Investors, actually,' Treasure corrected absently from his dressing room that adjoined their bedroom in Cheyne Walk. He was concentrating on knotting his bow tie.

The two were changing for a formal dinner party.

'All right, Investors. I'd prefer Attestors though. Sounds humbler.' The seated Molly studied herself in the mirror. 'Pearls, or diamond earrings with this dress?'

Treasure put his head around the dressing-room door. 'Mm . . . pearls.'

'No-o-o, I think the earrings.'

'Why ask then?'

'Because I value your opinion of course, darling. You haven't said why the Investors want the church.'

'Lots of reasons. Including one Smurt didn't mention this afternoon. On the surface, setting up in a church gives them a sort of instant credibility.' He paused. 'I seem to be low on white hankies.'

'You are. The ones your mother gave you two birthdays ago didn't wear at all well. Or you're blowing too hard.'

'Could you buy me some more?'

'Yes. Go on about the Investors and the church.'

'Well, again for them, Saint Martin's is in a specially good area. On the edge of central London, and fairly close to the BBC.'

'Because they'll want to poach staff from the Beeb?'

'Perhaps. Or because they'll need to be handy for free-lance people. Technicians, musicians, and so on.'

'Well in that case they can have me for dramatic Bible readings. They're rich enough, you said?' Molly picked up a bottle of scent, saw it was empty, put it back on the dressing table and searched for another.

'Of course, there are very few redundant churches in London that aren't protected for historical or architectural reasons,' Treasure ruminated, ignoring the last facetious suggestion.

'You mean they can knock Saint Martin's about with no one objecting?'

'Probably. They'll need to insulate it for sound and light, I suppose. And I imagine they'll need offices as well as permanent studios. All that could mean struc-tural changes inside, but without harming the outside much.'

'Until they get too big for the place. Then they'll sell it at a fat profit to someone who'll knock it down.'

Treasure emerged from the dressing room applying a clothes brush to the dinner jacket he was wearing. 'Ah, any development of that kind I think they'd do themselves.'

'Why d'you think that?'

'For another reason Smurt didn't offer for wanting the church. Thanks.' Molly had taken the brush and was doing the back of his jacket. 'After he left, I called an investment banker I know in Chicago. He was fairly informative, though he did caution that part of what he said was only rumour. The Investors have their headquarters in Chicago. They have a reputation for being highly successful in two important respects that have nothing to do with religion. First, they have a distinctly up-market membership, influ-ential in business. Secondly, they manage their investments very profitably, with large holdings in property as well as stocks and shares.'

'That's not my idea of an evangelising movement.'

56

'Perhaps not. The fact remains they're the only organisation of this kind with a significant young executive membership.'

'Upwardly mobile? And not just heavenwards,' Molly observed tartly, handing him back the brush and returning to her dressing-table.

'Yes. They've recruited an army of MBA's, apparently. Their leader, this Brother Jethro, he used to be dean of a business school. The investing they do is for the specific benefit of the members. That's their major purpose.'

'Not helping their neighbour? Doing unto others?'

'On the contrary, the members seem to be devoted to helping each other the whole time. In the business sense.'

'Like the Masons?'

'The way I read it, they could teach the Masons a lot about mutual aid.' He dropped into the bedside armchair.

'So it's a new twist?'

'In a way. It's a private company, but every paid-up member of the congregation is entitled to buy shares. The shares are valued daily against assets.'

'What kind of assets?'

'A go-go portfolio of public company shares, and another one in property. Their investment track record is pretty impressive. Of course, their market intelligence service comes through their own influential membership.'

'People at the top of industry?'

'In the main, not right at the top, but high enough up to be in the know when their companies are about to land contracts, or turn in high profits, or enjoy any special sort of success. And most particularly if they're about to get into a takeover situation.'

'Isn't that like insider trading? And isn't it against the law?'

'Certainly it is. Here and in America. But the law has to find the insider, and prove he or she benefited from using privileged information. In this case it's the Community of Investors for Jesus that benefits. Information goes anonymously into their pool of commercial intelligence. The organisation would probably plead the seal of the confessional if challenged about sources, assuming it admitted having any sources. That's the theory, but apparently it's never been tested. Also, as I said, a lot of this may be hearsay.'

'But if the members are more interested in material gain than they are in salvation, why join a church? Why not just use any information they get for private gain?'

'Because this way the individual benefits consistently through the scale of the thing. Much more, probably, than he would from exploiting the odd bit of insider information that comes his way. Far less risk of being found out as well.'

'So it works like a mutual fund?'

'You could say that, yes.'

'But why are they in property?'

'Because that's also an inside knowledge sort of business. The profits tend to take longer to build than with shares, but they can be very substantial.'

'And that's why the Investors are after Saint Martin's?'

'Almost certainly. That church is very valuable. Or more accurately, the church site. I think the Investors are starting the way they intend to carry on. That's if they're serious at all about extending what they call their congregation to Britain.'

'So why else would they come here?'

He shrugged. 'To widen their investments, cloaking that with a token effort at converting the natives. I mean tele-evangelising isn't really on in this country. People haven't bought satellite dishes so they can tune in to the likes of Brother Jethro.'

'Except you said Smurt is expecting changes in the law about religious programming.'

'And he's right. But I don't believe that makes the

viewers right. Mark you, he's better informed on a lot of things than he pretended. For instance, he didn't learn about the pending Saint Martin's redundancy from reading the porch notice board. He may even have known Aziz Developments are angling to buy the place. In that case, coming to Grenwood, Phipps for advice was very astute.'

Molly swivelled round to look at her husband. 'So if Aziz get the church, it'll be knocked down immediately, and if the Investors get it, it'll be knocked down a bit later.'

'That's about it.'

'Do you think Mrs Cudlum's protest movement will do any good?'

'It might. And one has the feeling deep down that it ought,' he added expansively, while looking at the time. 'Are you nearly ready?'

'Yes.' Molly turned back to the dressing table and began making faces at herself in the mirror. 'I'm glad you think that way about the protest. Mrs Lodey rang this afternoon. She asked if we'd go to the meeting with her tomorrow. If we were free. I said I thought we were. She's so sweet, and she really is potty about you.' Then, before he could reply, she added: 'You know, darling, you're right about these earrings. I'll wear the pearls instead.'

Chapter Six

'I mustn't be too late. Even though it's my night off. Mrs Lodey gets worried. About buggers, you see?' Miss Modd frowned. 'Muggers I mean,' she corrected loudly, amused not abashed by the error. She squinted keenly at the glass of champagne which she was holding quite close to her face, before electing to study it from a sideways angle, still with half-closed eyes. 'This champers is a grop . . .' She paused, drew breath, and began again. 'A drop of the good, all right,' she said, taking the words slowly and deliberately, like Eliza Doolittle under instruction in Shaw's *Pygmalion*.

'It sure isn't domestic. That's what we'd say back home,' Marvin Smurt agreed. He had been drinking very little – mostly only toying with his glass. It was his guest who had consumed most of the bottle between the start and the end of the meal, as well as the lion's share of the carafe of claret served with the main course.

'Domestic? Domestic? Oh, made here, you mean? You are a wag.' Miss Modd gave him a dig with her elbow that might have pitched a less formidable man off the narrow banquette they were both occupying. 'This is a jolly nice restaurant. In a jolly nice hotel,' she continued, smoothing a hand across her well-supported bosoms which were half exposed by the ruffed V-neck of her white evening blouse. Tonight she was affecting a determined if flamboyant appearance of femininity, in contrast to her normal style. She gazed about her, spreading approval on all sides, then took another substantial swig of champagne. Afterwards, her broad lips parted to exhibit a healthy pink tongue exercising itself in so languid a demonstration of bovine contentment as to put Smurt in mind of scenes from his Texan boyhood.

'More coffee?' he asked.

'Yes, please.' But it was her glass not her cup that she pushed forward. 'What was it you were saying about . . .' she concentrated hard as he poured the wine. 'About strategies?' She turned her face upwards to study his, frowned, and then drew back a little to adjust for focus on the monstrous moustache.

'That we should have Mrs Lodey appreciate that if the Investors move in, the church building stays,' said her lofty host.

'Won't get knocked down?' Miss Modd considered the point for a moment. 'Except the Investors aren't exactly your typical Church of England types. I gather that from what you said. Oh yes.'

She squared her shoulders, before thrusting her left hand boldly inside the blouse to rearrange a wayward strap.

Then suddenly, beneath the tablecloth, Miss Modd's right calf jambed itself hard against Smurt's left leg. The action was so abrupt, at first he felt it must have been a momentary reflex of some kind and not the product of a burgeoning need for greater intimacy.

Even so, her leg stayed where it was, tight against his.

'The fact remains, the Investors are dedicated Christians,' he offered, as though nothing had happened.

He decided that to withdraw his leg might seem in some way censorious, even though keeping it against hers involved playing a conscious pressure game beneath the table.

'Dedicated Christians. That's the ball point,' Miss Modd almost shouted. She was wearing an expression which could have indicated pain or suppressed passion. Her left hand was still inside her blouse but apparently frozen

61

there. 'I mean the bull point.' She gave a maniacal sort of chortle, before bringing the champagne glass to her lips – with immense concentration and only a slight wobble. 'Without the Investors, the developers will move in, and the church'll come down. Cradle and all.' She swallowed a mouthful of wine. 'Come down with a bloody great crash.'

At the end of all this, Miss Modd seemed to be seriously out of breath. Then her face welled up suddenly with relief. Her left hand emerged abruptly from the blouse, while at the same moment her leg ceased pressing against Smurt's.

With the need for below-table resistance so summarily ended, the surprised Smurt half fell upon his guest.

'I suppose you always stay in jolly nice hotels?' Miss Modd asked, more or less into his shirt front.

'Brother Jethro believes creature comforts are good for the soul. Within reason,' he answered, drawing back, and snapping his teeth together with a click that his companion found unnerving. He was aware that the two of them were becoming the object of sidelong glances from other diners, but decided to balance the embarrassment against the conviction that his corporate purpose was on the way to completion.

'Well here's to Brother Jethro,' said Miss Modd, lifting her glass with enthusiasm. 'My father – did I tell you he was in the Dragoons? – he used to have champagne with the dessert, too. Said it was good for the lib . . . the lib . . . the lib . . .'

She seemed to be stuck like the needle on a record player, and each new 'lib' got louder.

'The liberals?' Smurt guessed wildly.

'The libido,' Miss Modd completed instead, with bass response of true stereophonic quality at maximum volume, while outstaring the startled woman at the next table. 'My father knew all about the libido, and psychoanalysis. All that sort of thing. Unusual for a regular army officer. What are the bedrooms like here? Good are they? Got your own bathroom, I expect?'

'The rooms are fine.' He paused, aware that she was per-spiring rather freely. 'Would you like to see?' he enquired tentatively.

'You devil, Marvin. And why not?' She gave him another dig in the ribs. 'Well, if Brother Jethro wouldn't mind. We're both of mature years. Well I am. D'you know I'm fif . . . fort . . . ' She scowled. 'To tell the honest truth, I'll be fifty this year,' she ended with a compromise, while dabbing her neck with a dainty, lace-fringed handkerchief that was inadequate for the job.

'You could have fooled me, Charmaine.'

'I told you to call me Modd. Everyone does. And I was joking just now. About seeing your room. It was just curiosity. I wouldn't want to compromise you.'

'I have a suite.'

'A suite! I expect that's different. More coffee in the suite, then, before I leave for home.' Again she out-stared the woman at the next table before turning her attention back to the champagne and Smurt. 'So how exactly should we advise Mrs Lodey?'

'Right now, that it's in her interests to support the Investors. If developers get hold of the church, it'll be torn down for sure.'

'But what if the protest works? What if the church is kept the way it is? Not made re . . . not closed.'

'That can only happen if Mrs Lodey pays to have the roof repaired. And all the rest. She's the only one who can afford to do that. Everybody I've talked to thinks so. I guess Mr Treasure should believe that too.'

'We should make sure he does,' Miss Modd agreed vehemently.

'It'd mean Mrs Lodey laying out the kind of money we're happy to budget ourselves. That's if we get to care for the building. I'd be glad to show her the figures. I'd hate to see her carry that burden by herself.'

'Well, nobody else is going to help much,' Miss Modd nodded again. 'Mrs Cudlum will never raise real money.

Mrs Lodey could be bled dry. It'd be an outrage.' Then her expression changed to one of acute suspicion. 'But if the Investors get Saint Martin's, it won't be a church any more. It'll be a television studio.'

'A church *and* a television studio. There's a difference.' He pushed the table away, ready for them to leave.

'You're right, Marvin.' Miss Modd responded with vigour as though to confirm he had uttered a great profundity. The ball of her right hand descended on the uppermost part of his left leg, it just might have seemed by way of underlining comradely accord – except it was the banquette she had been aiming for and missed. She really had taken too much to drink.

The over-sensitive Smurt started violently. Unsure of what the hand was indicating, but fairly certain what it might be indicating to others, he pulled back the table swiftly. He'd had Miss Modd filed in his mind as a woman who didn't care for men.

'You're right, Marvin,' she repeated. While Smurt's opinion of her was loosening, her unintended grip on his taut anatomy was tightening – and only because she was preparing to heave herself into a standing position. 'Mrs Cudlum and her protest have to be stopped at all costs,' she pronounced, in the manner of someone taking a solemn oath.

The tall American relaxed a fraction, confident, at least, that whatever else followed, his prime object had been achieved.

'Someone said Molly Forbes thought you looked like a guards officer. When she saw you at the Sunday Club, remember? I think you're much nicer than that.' Caroline Tinder reached up while Peter Windle kissed her quite chastely on the lips.

'I suppose she meant it as a compliment,' he replied, grinning.

'Her husband, Mark Treasure, is awfully dishy. He was

terribly interested in everything too. They both were. I'll put your coat in the closet.' She had hung hers there already. Then she moved ahead of him through the hall of her parents' house and into the drawing room – with its chintz-covered chairs, and floral curtains which she went to close.

There was a Bechstein boudoir grand piano in the window bay. On both sides of the fireplace, antique glass cabinets displayed even more antique pieces of china and porcelain. A dull, over-large seascape hung above the mantelshelf. Invitation cards, in assorted sizes, some of the larger ones ponderously engraved, were threaded behind the bric-à-brac on the shelf below. A summons to a Buckingham Palace garden party was half obliterated by a much less distinguished card – an apparent touch of modesty, but effectively concealing that the garden party had taken place in the previous June.

'Coffee, tea, or . . . or me?' asked Caroline, blushing afterwards because she'd never said such a thing to a man before: she had only done so now because she was determined to sound more worldly than she was. Also, tonight she had definitely decided this man was going to be more important in her life than any other she had ever met. It had been their first formal date.

'I'll settle for you for the moment, thank you,' Peter answered. He was twenty-four, recently qualified, and looked as dashing as Molly Treasure had suggested. Even so, and less predictably than in Caroline's case, his previous amatory experience had been very limited. Thus, to this point, the evening had been as enjoyable as two young people nervous of each other had been able to make it. They had been to a film, and had supper afterwards at a local wine bar.

Now he wrapped his arms around her, and they kissed again, this time with more fervour. 'Your father won't mind my being here?' Peter asked later.

'No.' By mutual consent they had moved to sit on the

sofa in front of the fireplace: Caroline had turned on only one lamp near the door. 'Daddy isn't old-fashioned really. Nor Mummy. Anyway, they won't be back for ages.' It was just after ten-thirty.

'Only I got the feeling I upset them when I came before.'

'On Sunday? They'd been having an argument. Over the church. Nothing to do with you.'

Peter still looked doubtful. He had not stayed long on Sunday. He had been helping Caroline bring back some musical equipment from the church hall. It was then that they had arranged to see each other tonight. 'Is your mother still supporting the protest?'

'Not any more. Daddy got her round to his side in the end. He's determined the church should come down. As churchwarden, Mummy felt she had to be against at first. But I don't think she cared that much. Except you can never completely tell with Mummy. She doesn't always give in. But on such a public thing, she didn't like to look disloyal to Daddy. I suppose I shouldn't either.'

'Your mother used to be very keen on the Sunday Club.'

'That's the only thing, still. Since Daddy's on the borough council, she's been saying they ought to find some other place for the club if the church goes.'

'Shouldn't be too difficult.'

'Except, would you still help with the club, if you didn't live so close?'

'Probably not.' He and a lawyer friend, Denis Hite, who worked in the same company, shared one of the small, old houses near the church. 'And I hadn't intended going on with it anyway. Not in the summer. Not repairing furniture. I'm very bored with broken-down sofas.'

'But not this sofa?'

'It's hardly broken down. Not yet.' He took both her hands in his.

'Is your house on a short lease?'

66

'About ten minutes,' he joked. 'It belongs to the company. Denis and I rent it on an instant-notice-to-quit basis, until it's ready for demolition.'

'I thought you owned it between you,' she snuggled up closer.

'Wish we did. Or the ground it's on, anyway. I own about half the furniture. You really must come to see it soon.'

He had asked her before, but she had refused, implying her parents would not have approved. From her early teens, her relations with boys had been strictly circumscribed by her father, and she had used this as an excuse for avoiding having any – even until lately – though the real reason was her own shyness. Now she wished they had gone to Peter's house tonight.

'So the company can put you out when they like?'

'Yes. But the rent's very low. Nominal really. And they'll probably offer us another company place somewhere else afterwards. There are usually a few knocking about for footloose executives.'

'You work for a building company?'

'No. For a property developer. At the moment. Shall I kiss you again?'

'Yes, please.'

As her back arched, he slipped his hand under her sweater: she had nothing on beneath it.

'That's nice,' she murmured in his ear, when their lips parted. She kept her eyes closed as his hand moved to caress her breasts. 'I've never let anyone do this before. Does that make me a prude?'

'No. Only choosy. And you're not being a prude now,' he answered softly, kissing her again.

It was while they were locked in what both were finding an increasingly satisfying embrace that the door flew open suddenly.

The dinner-jacketed Lancelot Tinder burst into the room, snapped on several lights, stopped abruptly, then cleared his throat. 'Oh, it's you, Caroline. Good evening, Peter,' he said. 'Didn't know it was you two. We saw the light, though. You were so quiet. Thought you were burglars.' He had wanted to retreat to save embarrassment, but he had come too far to do so with any style. His wife was immediately behind him too – a place her husband regarded as appropriate for Enid Tinder in the order of things generally, not just when it would have been dangerous to let her go first.

'Good evening, sir.' Red-faced, the young man had shot to his feet. 'I'm sorry if . . . I mean, we've— '

'Hello, Peter, been to the cinema, have you? Caroline said you might. Good film? Had anything to eat?' Mrs Tinder, a homely woman in an equally homely, dark blue evening gown, bustled past her husband.

'Yes, Mummy. Super film. And we had supper in that wine bar. The one you like,' stammered Caroline who had also got up, after a frenzied effort to straighten her sweater.

'That's good. You might have put the fire on. Cheers things up.' Mrs Tinder bent to ignite the gas jet of an imitation log fire, similar to the one at Mrs Lodey's. 'It's colder tonight. Snow in the air. Or, perhaps you hadn't noticed.' She smiled knowingly at her daughter, before turning to puff up one of the cushions on the sofa.

'We didn't expect you back so soon,' said Peter, stating the obvious, then wishing he hadn't.

'The dinner we've been to in the City finished early. Main speaker cancelled at the last moment,' said Tinder, fingering his bow tie and beaming with forced bonhomie. He had very recently decided to encourage Caroline's ripening friendship with Peter Windle for several reasons. The young man was well qualified and had a promising job. More important, reference to *Who's Who* had revealed that his father was Sir Henry Windle, the noted industrialist.

Tinder had problems. Solutions might conceivably be

provided through important new acquaintances. It happened that Peter's employer had been recruited in just this guise some time ago, and he had not been found wanting.

'Our taxi driver was on the ball too,' Tinder went on. 'Got us home in record time.'

'Tea, coffee or anything else?' asked Mrs Tinder, and wondered why her daughter suddenly started to blush again.

'Tea would be nice, my dear,' said Tinder, ahead of the others. 'Unless you'd prefer something stronger, Peter?'

'Not for me, thanks,' Peter answered quickly, anxious at least not to qualify as a potential dipsomaniac as well as a daughter molester. 'Tea would be . . . I mean . . . Actually, I think I should be getting home,' he added, but making it sound more a question than a firm intention.

'Oh, must you? You've no distance to go. Why not stay for a cup?' Tinder encouraged.

'Of course he'll stay,' said his wife. 'Sit down all of you.'

'All right, thank you,' Peter replied. He and Caroline sat beside one another again on the sofa, a trifle self-consciously and with space between them. 'What happened to your dinner speaker, sir?' the young man asked earnestly, as though he really cared.

'Got the flu. Lot of it about,' said Tinder, dropping into an armchair. 'Quite a number of other guests cried off for the same reason.'

'Hope it won't stop people going to the Saint Martin's meeting tomorrow night,' said his wife. She was on her way out of the room.

'Good thing if it does,' snapped her husband, forgetting to be genial.

'Oh no. I still think people should have a chance to air their views,' Mrs Tinder replied, pausing thoughtfully for a moment in the doorway.

'Only if their views are worth anything.'

'Well, I still don't know how we can approve of a church

closing when we're always complaining about moral disintegration. Oh, don't worry, Lancelot, I'm not promoting the protest. Not any more.' Mrs Tinder smiled at Peter. 'I've given that up because my husband thinks it's infra dig. Even so, I think Angela Cudlum may have drummed up enough support to make the Bishop take notice.' With that she left the room to make the tea.

'I hope that's not true,' commented Tinder, selecting a long, straight, shiny pipe from a rack of other exactly similar ones.

'Mrs Cudlum's a strange lady,' said Peter. 'When her husband's about, you wouldn't think she was capable of saying boo to a goose. But when she's on her own she can be very noisy.'

'Is that so?' Tinder blew hard through the pipe stem.

'She can be obstinate, too,' Caroline put in.

'Well, I hardly know the woman.' Her father made it plain by the tone that he'd no desire to have that situation altered either.

'I'll just help Mummy with the tray,' said the girl, getting up.

There was a difficult silence after the two men were left alone in the room, though Tinder was making heavy going of filling his pipe.

'I . . . I'm sorry about when you came in tonight, sir.' Then for the second time in five minutes Peter wished he'd chosen to say something different: anything.

Tinder's left cheek twitched. 'No need to be. Caroline's quite young in many ways still, of course. I'm sure you respect that.'

'Of course, I— '

'Good,' the other interrupted dismissively. He struck a match. 'On this church business, I don't mind telling you I find any protraction in the matter very irritating.'

'I'm sure.'

'You know the Pastoral Committee was unanimous for redundancy? Quite unanimous.' Tinder sucked at the pipe as he spoke. 'Trouble is, I was on it. Probably a mistake, since I live in the parish – and in the square.' He looked up sharply. 'Not that anyone could doubt my objectivity. Been on plenty of Pastoral Committees in the past. It's work that needs experience and a lawyer's mind. In particular, it's essential one sees things in a wider than a mere parish context.' He pulled the pipe from his mouth and waved it for emphasis. 'The Archdeacon particularly asked me to sit on the Committee this year. Anyway, the sooner the Church Commissioners confirm our recommendation the better.'

'It's the Sunday Club more than anything else— '

'Yes. Case of the tail wagging the dog that is. Anyway, that's all taken care of. I spoke to the Borough Social Services Director myself about it.'

'Perhaps that'll be all right then. I shouldn't think the meeting tomorrow will make too much of a stir. Not really,' but Peter's ending was uncertain – though unintentionally so.

'You heard something that suggests the opposite?'

'Oh, no, sir,' Peter lied, because in the circumstances there was nothing else he could do.

'Good.' Tinder sat back contentedly with his pipe. 'So tell me, how's your celebrated chairman, Mr Aziz?'

'He's fine, I think.'

'Keeping you busy I expect?'

'Yes, very busy. I see him quite a lot. I mean considering I'm only a junior executive. Of course, the headquarters staff is quite small.'

'I see.' The speaker's eyes narrowed. 'Has he ever mentioned me in relation to the business, by any chance?' The enquiry was if anything over casual.

'No, sir.'

'No reason why he should, of course. We know each other, even so. Well, next time you run into him, tell him I enquired after him, won't you?'

Chapter Seven

The village high street in Cordley, Surrey is typically dead quiet and deserted at ten-thirty on a weeknight – and a Wednesday night in February at that time would be as typical as any. Through traffic uses the bypass, and few locals are on the street so late. Even so, the stone sent crashing through the window of the Full Moon Supermarket (country branch), and breaking the silence so dramatically, might have caused more of a stir than it did, at least in the nearby households.

Needless to say, it stirred the owners of the supermarket.

Sundar Frakraj heard the noise of the breaking glass a second before his wife's scream. He had been in the stockroom at the back. He dropped the case of soups he was lifting and raced into the shop, nearly toppling a bewildered looking elderly man, the only customer they'd had in for an hour.

'Mia, are you all right?' Frakraj couldn't see the check-out counter immediately. It was on the left, next to the street door. The centre merchandise aisle he was in was stacked high with groceries on both sides. 'Mia!' he called again, still running.

'I'm OK, Sundar,' she shouted as he came into view. She was holding onto the cash register – for support probably, not to protect the contents, though in a reflex way it might have been that too. Her face spelled terror.

'You're not hurt?' He grasped both her arms across the counter and felt her trembling.

'No, I'm not hurt. It's the other window. It's smashed.

72

Someone threw something. It was such a shock, I thought—'

'Did you see who it was?'

'No. How could I? My back's to the road.'

She was trembling still, and he sensed she was about to start crying. He squeezed her hands. 'There's no danger now. And you've been very brave. Can you manage to ring the police? Dial nine-nine-nine?'

She drew in breath sharply. 'Yes.' She reached for the telephone, then looked up again. 'Oh, Sundar, take care.'

But he'd pulled the door open and was outside already. He wasn't afraid. That kind didn't wait for a fight – or to be recognised. The street was empty, as he'd expected.

The shop had windows on either side of the door. It was the window to his right that had been holed. It wasn't a brick they'd used, but an uneven lump of concrete. He could see it lying inside on the floor, on top of a collapsed display of toilet-rolls, household detergents and cans of garden peas. It didn't matter what they'd used, of course. It was just that he knew smash-and-grab robbers used bricks: these people had been smashing but not grabbing. Otherwise he supposed they'd have gone for a jewellers, not a small general grocer's owned by a Sri Lankan.

Automatically the assailants were in the plural in Frakraj's mind, although there was no way he could know whether this particular outrage had been caused by more than one person. Simply, he classified the perpetrators as a sinister 'them' because it wasn't the first time something like this had happened.

Jagged bits of plate glass surrounded the uneven hole where the missile had gone through. In just a few more minutes the mesh shutters would have been in position. Perhaps they had known that.

A car went past on the other side of the street, slowed slightly, then sped on. There was a light in a window above one of the other shops in the row on this side, but there was no one looking out. The shops opposite and the living quarters above were all in darkness. People hadn't heard any noise, probably. Frakraj always gave the benefit of the doubt.

Both the two big outside displays of fruit and vegetables had been overturned, one completely so, the other only collapsed at one end, but the resulting wreckage was the same. There probably hadn't been time to tip over both displays completely, Frakraj mused grimly. Produce was scattered across the pavement, onto the road, and even as far as the other side. Some of the tomatoes had gone the whole distance, though most had stayed in the near gutter, incongruously stacking themselves there. Apples had done the same thing further along. He watched another lone car go by and squash an orange flat on the crown of the road.

He tried pulling one of the trestle tables upright but he couldn't manage it without stepping on plums and grapes. When he picked up a bruised melon, there was nowhere to put it.

'Get a grasp on yourself,' he admonished inwardly, but moving his lips to match the words. He sighed as he looked at the mess again. So, there was a big clearing up job to do, but he and Mia would need to do it methodically after the police had been. He shook his head slowly, staring now along the peaceful English village street. He would never understand why people in a civilised country could bring themselves to do such cruel things – but that was because he couldn't comprehend ignorant prejudice.

The elderly customer from inside the shop now appeared, clutching his raffia shopping bag. He was a frail figure in a worn-out overcoat who winced at the coldness of the outside air. Frakraj thought the old man would have sidled away if he could have done so without being noticed. As it was, he gave Frakraj a nervous look, straightened the flat cap he was wearing and said, 'Bit of a mess, isn't it then?' He frowned at the scattered produce on the pavement. 'The lady inside's all right.'

'Thank you,' said Frakraj.

'That's it then? You'll have the police along?' It was another way of saying. 'So you don't need me.' He stooped to pick up a stick of celery in his path, as a token of assistance, then looked about for somewhere to put it down. 'There's nothing I can do?'

'Nothing, thanks.' Frakraj took the celery, then pushed it into the old man's bag with the damaged melon that had still been in his hand. 'With my compliments. Give the celery a good wash, won't you? And thanks for your help.' It was best to do to others as you'd have them do to you.

The old man rubbed his nose and mumbled something that sounded like gratitude before shuffling away.

It was the waste that hurt Frakraj most. He would much rather have given all the food away than have it rolling about in the dirty road.

Mia was all right. That was the main thing. He was thinking that as the patrol car drew up. He had turned about at the sound of the engine, in time to see the near-side front wheel making instant tomato purée on a grand scale in the gutter, and driving it towards the drain.

'Anything like this happened here before, Mr Frakraj?' one of the two uniformed patrolmen was asking a few minutes later.

'Nothing as bad as this. We've had words painted on the window in the night. But that was some time ago. Before we had shutters fitted.'

'Was that reported, sir, d'you know?'

'Oh yes. At the police station.'

'I see. Anything else?'

'A nasty message pushed through the letter box once. With some . . . some dog mess. That was taken to the police station too. The note, not the dog mess.'

The young constable nodded, boot-faced, and made

another note in his book. 'You think it may have been a racist attack, sir?'

Frakraj smiled. 'Well, put it this way, officer. This is the only shop in the High Street not run by white people, and it's the only one that's had its windows broken, and the other things I mentioned. QED, wouldn't you say?'

'I see what you mean, sir.' This time the constable gave an embarrassed cough. 'Probably tearaways. There's no accounting for some of them.' He shook his head. 'And you don't live over the shop?'

'I don't, no, but Mr Shiv Singh does. He's my wife's brother. He and his wife Kiri are managing this shop for me. They're in Colombo, in Sri Lanka at the moment. Mrs Singh's mother is very, very ill. There is other help here during the day, but my wife and I are coming on some evenings, really to test whether it's worth staying open late.'

'And is it, sir?'

'Not really. Not so far as we can tell. We were going to stay till ten forty-five tonight. To see if there was any trade after the pubs closed.'

'It's nearly that time now, sir. You have another shop close by?'

'Not close. In West London. Kengrave Road. That's where we live. Fifteen miles north of here.'

'And you haven't had trouble like this in London, sir?'

'Nothing like this. Nothing at all. Well, not for a long time. Perhaps we're not so distinctive as here, officer?' Frakraj again proffered his indulgent smile. 'A good number of the shops around Kengrave Road are run by Asians.'

'Well, I think that'll do till the CID get here, sir.' The policeman put his notebook away. 'Let's give you a hand clearing up the worst of the mess. Then we'll see if we can get the place secured for the night.'

'That's very kind of you. Your colleague's started that already. And here's one of the many kind neighbours, as you can see.' He waved at a figure emerging from a doorway further along. 'I'm sure we'll manage things quite quickly. The steel blinds will work all right.'

But it was another three hours before Sundar and Mia Frakraj fell into bed in their London flat above the other shop in Kengrave Place, the alley to the north of St Martin's church.

The commercial and the living areas here were larger than the ones at the Surrey store, but much older and in poor condition. The shop abutted the church on one side, where both buildings faced Kengrave Road. At the rear, the flat overlooked the backyard of the vicarage and had a glimpse of the square. The private entrance to the flat was in Kengrave Place, beyond the side window to the shop.

The pair had come in and gone to bed quietly. This was to avoid waking either their small son Alan, or Frakraj's widowed mother who also lived with them.

'With that shop still losing money, and so far away, I don't know why we keep it on,' Mia complained now in a whisper, and still too upset to sleep. She was a pretty woman, petite, and much younger than her husband. Her long, straight black hair was always drawn back tightly from the high forehead. It was shining lustrously even now in the soft reflected light from the street.

Frakraj slipped an arm under his wife's waist. 'We've kept the shop because we all agreed the area had promise.'

'Except for the prejudice. Against Asians.'

'That's an overstatement. Like the policeman said, you can't legislate against tearaways.'

'It's more than tearaways. It's most of the people there, it seems to me. They don't use the shop. When it all happened tonight there was only one customer in. Only three or four all evening. Maybe the other shopkeepers have organised a boycott. Because we're open at night and Sundays. You know a lot of people think that's unfair competition.'

'Not at all. Mr Evans from the hardware store, he came to help tonight, didn't he?'

'He was the only one.'

'It was late when it happened. Probably the others were in bed.'

'You're too soft and forgiving.'

'And you're too shaken still. It was a nasty thing to happen. Very nasty.'

'Well I don't know how Shiv and Kiri stick it. I don't think Kiri wants to any more. She was saying so before they left for Colombo. And once we get the big new shop here we shan't need the other one in any case. The whole family can work here.'

'If we get the new shop. And that can't be for a long time, anyway. We need the other place till then at least. This one isn't big enough to support everyone as it is. Cordley will pick up in the summer, you'll see.' He drew closer to her. 'It takes time for strangers to be accepted, but the worst is over, I'm sure of that. It's always darkest before the dawn.'

She wriggled her bare body. It was not a sensuous, provocative gesture but one intended to show her disdain for his platitudes. 'And why should it be so long before we get the new shop? When we gave up the lease here— '

'We haven't given it up,' he interrupted. 'Not yet.'

'Good as, though?'

'Not really. We're part exchanging it for a lease on the new one they'll put up in its place. With compensation for loss of trade when they're rebuilding here. And a special price on a new flat,' he recounted carefully. 'That is the deal with Aziz Developments.'

'Plus somewhere for us to live while the building goes on?'

'That too, yes. It's a good deal. A very good deal.' He paused. 'If it comes off.'

'But once the church is pulled down— '

'Oh goodness me, my love, you must understand that's absolutely not certain yet. Not at all.'

'Shhh!' she scolded. 'Not so loud. You'll wake Alan. But deep down you think the church will go, don't you?'

He sighed. 'Yes. It's sad really.'

'But how can you say that when our future depends on it?'

'Only if it's God's will.'

Mia understood his fatalism less than she did his religion. They had both been brought up as Christians, but she had long since stopped going to church – and religion apart, she had never been one to leave to chance anything that could be positively affected in other ways.

'Anyway, there are plenty of other churches where you can play the organ,' she said.

'It isn't that. Destroying a church seems wrong. Mrs Cudlum is right to try stopping it.'

'But you're not supporting her?'

'I've said I'll go to the meeting.'

'But you haven't told anyone we'll benefit when the church goes? You don't have a conscience about that?'

'No. Because that can only happen— '

'Through God's will,' she broke in disparagingly. 'Well I hope you and God are on the same side. Because, I tell you, if it's a case of my family's future and Mrs Cudlum's romantic notions, then Mrs Cudlum can go to hell with my help. So there.'

'I said, will you be coming to the meeting tonight, Nigel?' Angela Cudlum repeated nervously the next morning. She was sitting across from her husband at the kitchen table. All the muscles in her body tightened as she waited to see if he would answer.

The Reverend Nigel Cudlum lowered his copy of *The Times* and stared blankly at his wife before turning a livelier gaze onto his empty cup. 'I'd like more coffee.' He continued to study the cup until she took it: there was nothing else that merited his attention.

It was an uninspiring room. She had painted the walls

herself a year before – in an off-white colour that her husband had criticised afterwards as impractical. The fitments couldn't have been changed for several decades, not the cooker, nor the refrigerator, nor the twin-tub washing machine. The stone sink and wooden draining board were probably half a century old. There were no built-in storage units, only open shelves and some free-standing cupboards of differing designs and heights. There was an old-fashioned range that Mrs Cudlum kept blackleaded. The range hadn't been used since the diocese had paid for the vicarage to be centrally heated some years before the Cudlums had arrived.

As always, breakfast had been an unbalanced affair. The Vicar had consumed eggs and bacon, while his wife had eaten only toast. If asked she would have insisted she didn't care for a cooked breakfast, but that wouldn't have been true. Simply, her housekeeping money wouldn't have stretched to such luxury for both of them.

Angela Cudlum got up and made her husband another cup of coffee – measured carefully from the tin of 'instant' by the electric kettle on the draining board.

In his previous job, at the university, he had gone into college each morning for a subsidised breakfast in the refectory. He had taken most of his other meals there too in term time, so that he'd had less occasion to notice how little Angela ate, and how badly. It was possibly why he had stopped noticing at all when they moved to St Martin's, even when she served him meat and ate only vegetables herself. At the back of his mind the convenient notion had formed that Angela had become some kind of vegetarian. He had never taxed her on the point. In any case, he tended to overlook trivia.

'About the meeting, Nigel. You *are* coming? It'll mean a lot to me if you're coming.'

He winced inwardly as she repeated the word 'coming' with that penetrating Midland accent of hers – as if it was spelled 'cumbing', or as if she had a permanent cold, or both. It grated with him more than any other word she used, probably because she used it so often. It was only in recent years that her accent had bothered him.

'You know my views on your misguided protest, Angela.' He fingered the edge of his goatee beard which, combined with the strong nose and mouth, and the full head of carefully waved and exquisitely trimmed hair put many in mind of a Holman Hunt portrait of the Saviour: it put Nigel Cudlum in mind of that too.

'There's nowhere else for the Sunday Club. If the church goes, it could be that'll have to go too,' said Angela.

He sighed. At first she thought that would be his only response, until he said. 'You're not still pushing that as the sole reason for maintaining the church?'

'Not the sole reason. No. But those people have nowhere else to go. Especially in winter. They've come to rely on the Club.'

There was that 'cumb' of hers again. 'And how many times must I tell you, the local authority will have to make arrangements to cope? As it should have done before? The Church of England isn't a welfare organisation.'

'Don't you think it should be, Nigel? Partly? They're saying if you of all people don't oppose the redundancy, no one else will.' Underneath the table she was clasping and unclasping her hands, willing herself to say her piece in the way she had practised while lying awake in the middle of the night.

'The Church of England is concerned for the salvation of your immortal soul, not the comfort of those freeloaders at the Sunday Club. And who are we to question the considered judgement of the Bishop and the Archdeacon? Not to mention the Church Commissioners? They're not all idiots, you know?'

'But I don't think they look at things from the parish level.' She kept her eyes fixed on her bread plate.

'Of course they do. But they also have to view them

in a wider perspective. Precisely what I shall have to do in Salchester.'

She looked up sharply as much in hope as in surprise. 'They're not going to close the cathedral?'

'Don't be ridiculous.' He wondered sometimes if she was getting to be feeble-minded.

He never made allowance for the strain she felt in opposing him in anything, or for the deepening sense of inferiority she had developed in her relationship with him. He had grown too far away from her to be aware of anything so much as that she had become a drag on his career – though that was an awareness he had not hesitated to let her share. 'Anyway, Saint Martin's isn't our problem any more,' he went on, a touch less harshly. 'You should be working on how to make your mark in Salchester. Just as I am. You can do it, you know? If you try.' He watched her face, hoping she wasn't going to cry. But she had to come to terms with reality at some moments in her life.

'I don't want to go to Salchester,' she almost whispered.

'Nonsense.'

'I shan't fit in. I know it.' She looked up at him. As he'd feared, tears were beginning to cloud her eyes. 'You know it, too. It was bad enough at the university.'

Except in his last job she had at least had time for paid work of her own – not very well paid, but it had given them extra income and her some small fulfilment. Being a London vicar's wife had proved to be a full-time job on its own, though unpaid. She was certain that she would be as unsuited to filling a spouse's role in a cathedral close as she had been to doing the same thing on a university campus, and possibly without the solace of doing a job of her own.

For a moment their gazes locked in what an outsider might easily have taken to be total disdain on his part, confronting near-despair on hers. And an outsider did join them, unheralded, at that very moment.

'Morning both. The back door was open. Did you

know? Can I have the key to the church hall?' It was Kate Garely who had burst in. Her flat was two streets away. She was looking fit and unusually fetching in black leggings under a short woollen street coat. 'Cheer up. It's sunny outside, even though there's snow forecast. Are you coming to aerobics this morning, Angela?'

'I don't think I can. Not this morning. I don't feel up to it, and I've such a lot to do.'

'Well, I think she should, don't you Kate?' This was Cudlum who had stood up. He kissed the visitor warmly on the cheek, and with less of the appearance of conveying a chaste blessing than when he greeted other women members of the parish in this way. 'Half a mind to come myself,' he went on, eyeing the visitor with a grin. 'Want some coffee?'

Angela was glad Kate had arrived. Her friend had the effect of humanising her husband to a degree Angela never expected to achieve again – always supposing she had ever done so.

'No coffee thanks.' Kate had moved across to Angela. 'What's the matter, poppet? You worried about the meeting? Nigel, you are going to be there?'

'Sadly, I can't. The Chaplain at University College went down with the flu yesterday. I've promised to stand in and give one of his Lent lectures tonight.'

Angela caught her breath, but otherwise disguised her surprise by picking up some dirty plates and turning sharply toward the sink. It wasn't the half-expected rejection – only that he could so easily have told her the same thing earlier, instead of making her plead to no purpose.

'Well I suppose that gets you off the hook, Nigel,' said Kate breezily, helping Angela with the dishes. It was something Angela would never have dared say to him, even though she had been thinking it.

'That's not quite fair,' Cudlum answered, but without any hint of rancour.

'It's perfectly fair. It's quite beastly of you to have

got drafted to do some dreary Lent lecture. Just because you're a brilliant academic. It wouldn't have hurt you to support Angela's last stand.'

'Well, probably I would have, if it hadn't been for this emergency. Even though it's a lost cause.' He looked at his wife as he spoke, wondering if she believed him, and not caring very much either way. He had appreciated Kate's compliment which had more than cancelled out her criticism. He wondered how Angela would cope at all if her friend was not around to stand up for her.

Angela breathed in hard. 'It's not a lost cause, you know? And Kate, it's not my last stand either.' Then, on the brink of tears, she hurried from the room.

After a pointed glance at Cudlum, Kate followed her.

Chapter Eight

'So that's forty-eight in favour. Nineteen against. Motion carried,' said Mr Rickit, the chairman of the meeting, but finishing with less absolute certainty than the count would seem to have justified.

The elderly Rickit adjusted the control of his hearing-aid again, thankful that the count had not been challenged. He was having difficulty enough locating the audience at all, let alone counting the raised hands: he had come out with the wrong glasses. He was seated, between Angela Cudlum and a spotty-faced, gangling young man, at a long trestle table perched precariously on a rather small platform. The young man was called Nottel, and he had volunteered at the start to take the minutes.

Rickit and Nottel were both members of the St Martin's Parochial Church Council. Even so, it had been stressed earlier that the gathering tonight wasn't a formal parish meeting since, by law, that would have required more notice than had been given.

There had been an official meeting to debate the redundancy question six months before this. Only seventeen people had turned up to it, strengthening the opinion of Lancelot Tinder, who had been there, that the church could be closed with hardly anyone really minding. Neither Mr nor Mrs Tinder was in evidence now, though their daughter was – in the fourth row with Peter Windle.

The present meeting had resolved very little so far. To begin with, it had been too unstructured. Angela Cudlum had made a convincing opening statement, but, after that, she and the other organisers seemed to have relied too much on emotion to carry things through, and too little on a purposeful agenda. More to the point, they hadn't expected opposition.

Mark Treasure shifted in his not very comfortable plastic chair. 'There were five fewer abstentions that time. Sixty-two voted on the previous motion,' he remarked to Molly who was beside him.

'Does that matter?'

'Not in the least,' he admitted blandly. 'Don't know why I mentioned it.' He had made the calculation simply to relieve the boredom and the burgeoning frustration. Captains of commerce who attend meetings of this kind intending, for whatever reason, to remain observers, usually succumb to exasperation in the end. Treasure was proving no exception on this occasion. He had ceased wondering why he had agreed to come at all and was concerned only about how soon he would be allowed to leave. Once more he looked about the room which was now more a stuffy basement and less a lively, multi-purpose church hall than when he had last been here. The card tables, the recycled sofas, the table-tennis equipment, and everything else easily movable had been stored around the refreshment area, making room for twenty or so rows of chairs facing the platform at the opposite end.

The Treasures were in the second row. Mrs Lodey was on the banker's other side, sitting bolt upright, and listening intently, with hands clasped before her over the silver handle of her cane. Miss Modd was beside her. She had arrived behind the others, and unexpectedly, since her employer had previously reported that she was indisposed.

Only one of the eight chairs in the front row was occupied – by Kate Garely.

The attendance of around seventy people had been bigger than Treasure had expected, particularly since it had been snowing from mid-afternoon. He was as surprised as the organisers that some of those present had evidently come to support the closure of the church, not to campaign to keep it open. He wondered again if Marvin Smurt intended saying anything. The American had arrived just after the meeting had started, and though he was seated near the back, a stranger of his height and presence could hardly pass unnoticed, or fail to engender an expectancy. He had waved warmly to Treasure, as if greeting an old acquaintance.

'Through you, Mr Chairman, can I ask Mrs Cudlum if she's going to take the petition round the parish for signing?' asked a middle-aged woman in a black beret.

The last resolution, and there had been many, had been to approve the words of a petition to be sent to the Bishop, and to the Church Commissioners, signed by everyone who was in favour of the church staying open. It wasn't anything the meeting need have voted over, except that the anti contingent – a clear though vociferous minority – had forced 'a democratic show of hands' on this and most other issues from the start, including one about who should be chairman.

'Yes, I'll be taking it round the parish,' replied Angela, holding up a copy of the petition she had prepared ahead of the meeting. There were a number of signatures on it already: the opposition had registered indignation about that earlier. 'There'll be extra copies for others to use,' she added.

'And will you be sure all the names on it are people who live in the parish?' called a man with a sing-song accent from the back – a voice that had been raised in opposition before.

'That's the man Jones again. He's a Welsh plumber, and an indifferent one at that,' Mrs Lodey vouchsafed to Treasure without looking round to confirm her conjecture.

'He owns one of the old end houses, and stands to

profit from it,' Miss Modd supplemented in a voice loud enough for almost all to hear.

'The petition can be signed by anybody,' countered Angela, to a chorus of 'hear, hear'.

This was a very different Angela Cudlum from the one put down so often that morning by her husband. She was not cowed by nature – only by Nigel Cudlum.

'But that's not right, is it, Mr Chairman?' called Jones again, this time standing. He was fifty or so, small, dark, and moon-faced, wearing steel-framed spectacles and a bright red sweater. 'It didn't ought to be signed except by parishioners,' he went on. 'Or by certified members of the electoral roll.'

'It's you needs certifying,' a Cockney voice countered in exasperation.

'Order,' called the chairman, in response to the loud murmurs of approval that followed the last popular comment. The majority was now definitely getting irked by the anti faction who many had now concluded were present under false pretences.

'I'd like to know why the petition shouldn't be signed by non-parishioners?' Angela demanded.

'Because it'll give a biased impression to the Bishop of what's the real opinion in the parish,' offered a female voice close to Jones, and in a Welsh accent that matched his.

'Nonsense,' Angela retorted. 'People who think that way should organise their own petition.'

'That's right.' This was Kate Garely, in support from the front row. 'Plenty of people come to the church from outside this parish. Always have. They're entitled to register their opinion the same as anyone else.'

There was more noisy approval for this, drowning out cries of dissent.

'Only five from outside the parish came to church last Sunday morning. To the eleven o'clock, that is. And three of them are on the official electoral roll,' countered

Jones, as soon as he could be heard, and thriving on the controversy.

'We must have been the other two. How observant of him,' whispered Molly to her husband.

'You're too easily identified. You should wear dark glasses,' he answered, summoning a grin.

'I don't live in the parish,' a frail old lady in a felt out-door coat offered breathily, from one of the middle rows. 'My friend Mavis don't neither. She's not 'ere tonight. Bilious attack. But we're reg'lar at Saint Martin's. Reg'lar as clockwork we are.' A solid phalanx of frail old ladies in outdoor coats around her were all now nodding their heads at each other, and at the chairman.

'Regulars at the Sunday Club whist drive don't count as churchgoers,' came a disparaging male voice from the back, not Jones this time.

'Give over, mate. We're regulars, and we never touch flipping cards, neither,' cried Kevin Hawker, a brawny youth with green hair, and dressed in jeans. He had a gold ring through one ear. Treasure remembered him as one of the sofa repairers.

There was a fresh roar of assent.

'Order,' called the chairman, gazing accusingly it seemed at the tea urn.

'Kevin's right,' shouted Marlon Barclay, a curly-haired black youth, also jeaned and earringed. 'Sunday Club OK. OK?' He jumped up, brandishing clenched fists and look-ing about him menacingly. The response to this was less certain than before, particularly from the old ladies. Even so, it was obvious that while the pro-redundancy group had come organised, Sunday Club members were ready to be counted too, though they had been less forward to this point.

'Order,' called the chairman again, and when he thought he'd got it, went on: 'I really don't see how any-one can object to Mrs Cudlum getting signatures from non-parishioners. Nor why non-parishioners shouldn't be allowed to campaign for the church. And if they come to the Sunday Club—'

'It's the principle, Mr Chairman,' a voice interrupted from the back.

'No it's not. Of course any outsider should be allowed to sign,' Kate Garely countered hotly, swinging around in her seat.

'If I could be allowed to comment—' began Nottel, the minute-taker, while leaning back from that task. But whatever it was the lanky young man intended to say was never uttered because he then completely disappeared from view. His tilted chair had slipped off the back of the narrow platform.

'Do it again, Nottel,' called Marlon Barclay, squirming with delight.

'We didn't see, Nottel,' the other youths from the Sunday Club took up with great good-humour, and unconcerned about whether the frail subject of their derision had done himself an injury.

'Order,' pleaded the chairman, wondering where Nottel had gone until that unfortunate came clambering back onto the platform with his chair, apparently unscathed, and to shouts of congratulation from the others.

Smiling sheepishly, Nottel gave a faltering wave to the audience, and sat down again. He made no attempt to restart his statement.

Protectively, Rickit pulled his own chair closer to the table.

Mrs Lodey raised her eyebrows at Treasure.

Angela Cudlum cleared her throat.

But it was Mia Frakraj who spoke next. 'Well, I'm against people outside the parish having a say in any of this. It won't be their responsibility if the church roof falls in, will it?' she demanded without rising. She was sitting beside her discomfited husband in the row behind the Treasures. Frakraj himself had said nothing so far, and was clearly wishing his wife hadn't either.

'In practice, that wouldn't be the responsibility of the parishioners either,' Angela answered gently from the platform, to a general murmur of agreement. 'I think the insurance covers anything of that kind.'

'Well, it ought to be the responsibility of the parishioners. Otherwise it don't make any sense, does it?' piped up Jones again. 'If the parishioners don't care, and don't have to, there shouldn't be a church.'

'The church is dedicated to the glory of God,' tremoloed Mrs Lodey suddenly and to huge dramatic effect. 'That is a sufficient reason for the existence of any church.'

'That is quite right,' agreed Sundar Frakraj, breaking the awed silence that followed.

' 'Ere, 'ere,' called earringed Marlon, elbowing earringed Kevin who called the same.

'I was going to say earlier, Mr Chairman,' began Nottel from the platform.

'Do it again, Nottel,' a young voice chanted, followed by some catcalling that stopped when Marlon ordered: 'Shurrup'.

'Order,' cried the chairman, at this point unnecessarily, while bringing a hand down hard on the table, and upsetting a glass of water straight into Nottel's lap.

'I was going to say,' Nottel repeated above renewed cheering, while ineffectively mopping at his trousers with a handkerchief. But this time he was determined to continue despite calamity. 'The insurance company won't give us cover on the building any more. That's after the policy comes up for renewal in April. Not unless the immediate structural defects are made safe before then, and work put in hand for major repairs.'

'Mr Chairman, is the Archdeacon aware of this?' asked Treasure crisply, standing up to speak, and no longer able to remain silent, or to endure the waffling and the indecision.

'Yes, sir, he is.' It was Nottel who replied after a nod from Rickit.

'Mr Nottel is parish treasurer, Mr Treasure,' provided Angela Cudlum.

'And presumably the Diocese is prepared to authorise the work?' This was Treasure again.

'And to lend us the money,' said Nottel. 'For the minimum work. To stop anything dangerous. Even that's going to cost more than ten thousand pounds.'

'I'd like to say something on that, Mr Chairman.' It was Smurt at the back, rising to his feet, and looking to those seated as if his head would just about brush the ceiling. 'My name is Marvin Smurt. I'm a humble office holder in the Community of Investors for Jesus in the U S of A. We heard about your problem here. And we prayed about it.' He bent his head reverently, then lifted it again. 'And maybe it was our prayers, plus your prayers, that helped bring us to a possible solution. And that's why I'm here with you tonight.'

Most heads were now turned in Smurt's direction. The assertion that total strangers had been moved to prayer over the present difficulty produced a variety of facial expressions, ranging from the firmly pious to the frankly dubious.

'We're a Christian community, Mr Chairman.' Smurt warmed to his theme. 'With solid Christian aims. We preach the gospel. The old gospel, but in the new way. We're television evangelists.' He held up his hand. 'And before you kind of dismiss us for that. Before you recall all the reports and mis-reports about tele-evangelists, let me say you can dig as deep as you like, and you'll come up with nothing but good news on the Community of Investors for Jesus. You'll also find we have considerable resources to put at the Lord's command. Mr Mark Treasure, Chief Executive of Grenwood, Phipps the merchant bankers, will maybe confirm that.'

He paused, and looked at Treasure. But the banker was irritated at the cavalier way his goodwill was being contrived, and showed as much in his silence and in his face.

'Thank you,' Smurt continued unabashed, just as though Treasure had done what had been asked. 'What we have in mind is to take over responsibility for this sacred temple to the Lord. To buy it, then to mend it. To heal its wounds. To put it back to work. Back to the Lord's work. May God bless you all.' With that gratuitous entreaty he sat down again.

'What do you expect to get out of it, then?' asked Jones cheekily, above the general chatter that followed – and for once he seemed to have the sympathy of most of the audience. 'Leave it as a church would you? Church of England? Like it is now?'

Smurt got to his feet again. 'Through you, Mr Chairman, in answer to our good friend here, we expect many things. We expect to bring the word of the Lord to thousands, maybe millions who long to hear it. We expect to renew the spirit of Christian hope and service in the hearts, minds and bodies of all who come to worship in and through this building.' He paused to gauge reaction, which was rather more hung than evident, before he resumed at a quickened pace. 'Without altering the outside of the structure one bit, we also expect to convert some part of the inside of Saint Martin's into a recording studio. Not just another recording studio, you understand? Not a commercial recording studio. Saint Martin's could become the headquarters of Investors for Jesus in Europe.'

'That,' Mrs Lodey exclaimed, producing an immediate expectant hush. 'That it will certainly never be.'

'That's right, Mrs Lodey,' roared Jones.

' 'Ere, 'ere,' affirmed the earringed brigade.

The whist-drive ladies clapped in support, along with everyone else.

Whatever effect Smurt had expected from his grandiloquent pronouncements it wasn't that he would have united virtually the whole audience in opposition to himself.

'I'm sure we're grateful to have heard from Mr Smart,'

began the embarrassed chairman. Nottel whispered something in his ear. 'I'm sorry, Mr Shirt. But what he has in mind is a little unexpected—'

'What he has in mind isn't on, Mr Chairman,' Jones had interrupted. 'When the church is closed, it won't be handed over to religious loonies. It'll be knocked down so dwellings can be built for the homeless.'

'Don't you mean flats at half a million pounds each for the rich?' countered Angela from the platform. 'With people who own nearby property ready for development cashing in at the same time?'

Heavy audience backing for this bold statement was immediate.

'That's not fair. Not fair at all,' protested Jones in a hurt voice, and in turn generating his own support.

'Yes it is fair,' exclaimed Miss Garely above the ensuing tumult.

'Order,' demanded Rickit as a matter of course.

'This meeting was called about keeping Saint Martin's the way it is. And it's time we were coming back to that, Mr Chairman,' Angela Cudlum put in shrilly, with a 'cumbing' that would have withered her husband. 'I said at the start, if we want our church to stay open, we first have to say so forcefully to the powers that be. We're doing that with the petition. We'll get two thousand signatures, I guarantee, and that should be enough. Then we have to put our money where our mouths are, and find the three hundred thousand pounds to cover the repair bills. We can't do that by ourselves, that's obvious. But if we organise, there are plenty of extra sources.'

'When you're in Salchester, Mrs Cudlum?' a woman's voice questioned from near the back.

'That's right, Mr Chairman.' This was Jones, standing to speak. 'What's the point of the Vicar's wife whipping up feeling for a lost cause? She leaves the parish in a week or two.'

'Mr Chairman,' Angela hesitated, blinked several times,

then began again. 'Mr Chairman, I'll . . . I'll not leave. I'll stay while there's hope of us succeeding.' She swallowed awkwardly as though on the enormity of what she had just said, then her head lifted and she stared about the audience with a look that was both determined and defiant.

'That's a big decision,' Molly Treasure said to her husband.

'Staggeringly so,' Mrs Lodey commented, catching Molly's words.

'Three cheers for Mrs Cudlum,' the boisterous Marlon called above the clapping, waving his arms about.

'Ord— ' began the chairman, but it was unnecessary for him to continue.

Mrs Lodey had risen slowly. Now she stood, erect and aristocratic, a parched and aged beauty in a long fur coat and a dainty black hat. She waited until the silence she had commanded was not merely complete but also acutely deferential.

'Mr Chairman. This church was erected at the instigation of my grandfather, the late Algernon Bertram Arbuthnot Grenwood, out of Christian charity, his love of God and for his fellow men.'

She paused, some thought while she decided whether to include fellow women as well – except Monica Lodey stemmed from an age when people of sound upbringing would have considered such an inclusion as superfluous, and possibly libellous.

'He did not count the cost. In his example and memory neither shall I, at this critical time,' Mrs Lodey continued, her voice seeming to strengthen with use, so that the frequent changes in register and modulation took on an expressive quality closer to music than to speech. 'I have consulted my grandfather's diaries from the relevant period. In response to the earnest entreaties of the future parishioners, he donated the land for the church outright. As for the cost of building, the church and the vicarage, he undertook to provide twice the sum raised by public subscription toward the work. That was his only condition. I consider it to have been a wise and prudent one.'

Mrs Lodey shifted on her feet, tapping the end of her stick between them. 'I am much moved by Mrs Cudlum's plan, her dedication, and the sacrifice she is ready to make to a cause she has made her own. I believe she deserves to succeed. To this end, in emulation of my dear grandfather, and in his memory, I undertake to subscribe two pounds for every one donated to the restoration fund from all other sources. The sum will be covenanted to save tax in whatever way the accountants prescribe. Naturally, this is on the understanding that the church remains open as a church, un . . . unmutilated.' She cast about for a sight of Smurt, fixing him with a brief, disapproving glower before adding, 'And that the Bishop appoints an incumbent to replace Nigel Cudlum who is leaving us.'

Cheering broke out as Mrs Lodey resumed her seat with great dignity.

'Thank you, Mrs Lodey,' said the chairman when the noise had stopped. 'I'm sure all of us, that is, all of us who want the church to continue, are deeply in your debt already.'

'The offer's magnificent, Mrs Lodey,' added Angela Cudlum, tears of joy in her eyes. 'We won't let you down.'

'Mr Chairman?' Molly Treasure was now on her feet. 'As someone deeply moved and interested, although from outside the parish, I'd like to open the subscription to Mrs Cudlum's fund with a donation of five thousand pounds. You'll have no problem accepting it, I hope. Nor my signature on the petition? Oh, and my name is Molly Forbes.'

'No problem at all, Miss Forbes. Or should I say Mrs Treasure?'

'You can if you like. My husband and I have been legally married for many years,' Molly smiled and sat down.

Frakraj sprang up immediately. 'Mr Chairman, I am Sundar Frakraj and I would like to give one thousand pounds,' he said, resuming his seat again quickly.

'Oh dear, Sundar, you've gone mad,' said his wife as the chairman offered thanks.

In a few minutes over twelve thousand pounds was pledged. Some of the larger contributions – none so large as Molly's or even Frakraj's, but substantial – came from the more conservative though often not the most affluent-looking members of the audience. Mostly, these were people who had said nothing in the debate. At the same time as they pledged money, all of them volunteered to collect signatures for the petition.

It was during a lull after this that Peter Windle got up, and approached the platform. There he had a whispered conversation with the chairman and the other two at the table, before returning to his seat beside Caroline Tinder.

The aged Rickit cleared his throat. 'Ladies and gentlemen, Mr Windle has raised a very good point. He's a qualified accountant. Although we have twelve thousand pounds promised already, that's thirty-six thousand if you add Mrs Lodey's contribution,' – he bowed in the general direction of the lady – 'it still has to be accepted these pledges of money and any others we collect won't necessarily be exercised. Not unless the diocese withdraws the application for redundancy.'

'Why not?' called someone.

Rickit's face clouded. 'Perhaps Mr Windle would like to explain?'

Peter stood up. 'Because Mrs Lodey's made it clear her magnificent offer depends on the church staying open,' he said. 'And in any case, it wouldn't be fair. Not for anyone to give, in the belief the church is going to be kept going as a church. Not if, after the money's subscribed and spent on repairs, the church is then closed. You'll have to get the Bishop's word first.'

'You and Mrs Lodey can have the word of the Investors for Jesus right now, Mr Chairman,' said Smurt, rising promptly and sounding to be a long way from defeat. 'If the Investors for Jesus are eventually charged with the safekeeping of Saint Martin's, anyone contributing to the repair fund in the meantime will get their money back. I've already said, we'll be happy to pay for the repair work ourselves, and then some.'

'With respect, Mr Chairman, for Mr Smurt to say that is meaningless.' This was Nottel trying to look stern. 'If his organisation gets the safekeeping of the church, as he puts it, the redundancy notice won't have been withdrawn, and the church will already have been closed down. So the money pledged tonight, and any more Mrs Cudlum is offered, won't have been collected. Or spent.'

'Are we splitting hairs, Mr Chairman?' asked Treasure rising, foreseeing a long and purposeless debate about the obvious, and anxious to get on. 'In the circumstances, it's clear you shouldn't call in the money unless the diocese withdraws the closure notice.'

Despite the optimism, on resuming his seat the banker thought it unlikely the parishioners and others could raise a third of the sum needed, and that Mrs Lodey would ever need to match that with the other two-thirds.

But without the money being subscribed, it was equally unlikely the diocese was going to withdraw the redundancy notice. This made the whole affair comparable to the question about which came first, the chicken or the egg.

As Treasure saw it, on balance, Aziz Developments remained the likeliest victors, with the Investors for Jesus a poor second, and the parishioners nowhere. Even so, he was much impressed with Angela Cudlum's sincerity and dedication. Nor was he the only one present who considered she might have the power to work a minor miracle.

'I think Mr Treasure's right,' said Angela now. 'It makes the petition really just as urgent as the money. I'll aim to have those names by the end of the next week. Duplicates of the petition will be ready first thing in the morning from the vicarage. That's for people who've offered to make house calls for me. I need more time to organise the collection of pledges. That'll do after we've seen the Bishop with the petition.'

'Good note to end the meeting on, I think,' said Rickit, looking tired. 'We have a great champion in Mrs Cudlum. Let's leave her to lead us to victory.'

Chapter Nine

'The whole thing is totally irresponsible,' said Lancelot Tinder, sucking hard on his pipe and glaring accusingly at the simulated burning logs in the fireplace of his drawing room. 'Mrs Lodey hasn't listened to a word I've said to her. Obviously I was wasting my time and my breath.'

'She's emotionally involved because of her grandfather, Daddy. It's rather sweet really,' Caroline replied.

'Wouldn't have been sweet if I'd been there.'

'Perhaps you should have been, dear. And so should I,' offered his wife gently, without looking up from her knitting. She glanced at her watch. 'Goodness, it's nearly time for the television news. Why didn't Peter come back with you, Caroline?'

'Work to do, poor lamb. Had to make a phone call to Los Angeles, he said. Sounded terribly important. I think he only came to the meeting to please me. He was very good. Over what he said at the end.'

'So you explained, dear,' her mother smiled knowingly, then nodded at her husband opposite, except he was still looking daggers at the fire.

It was nearly ten o'clock. The church meeting had finished twenty minutes or so earlier.

Caroline hadn't admitted her disappointment about Peter not coming in with her – or, better still, inviting her back to his house: she had dropped a big enough hint about that. In the end she had accepted his plea about work, because it saved face. Deep down she was afraid he might be getting tired of her already – that she hadn't been passionate enough or something the evening before. When he had walked her across the square he had seemed worried or preoccupied – or bored perhaps?

For the first time, the nineteen-year-old Caroline was suddenly very much in love, and very insecure about it. Bizarre notions were going through her mind, including the idea that Peter might have been intending to see some other girl after he'd left her. It had been quite early still. Even when he'd kissed her goodnight in the doorway it had lacked the keenness of last night. True, they had both been wrapped up against the weather, though the snow had stopped and a thaw started by then. Even so, it's difficult to be hot-blooded through two topcoats.

'Sorry, Daddy, what did you say?'

'I said how can Mrs Cudlum be planning to stay here? After her husband goes to Salchester Cathedral? I find that very difficult to credit.'

'The vicarage will be empty, of course,' put in Mrs Tinder.

'That's not the point,' he came back abruptly. 'She should be with her husband. It's her duty.'

'Not all modern wives—'

'And she'll have no legal right to live in the vicarage, in any case,' he interrupted.

'But if no new vicar's being appointed . . .' Mrs Tinder paused, choosing her next words carefully because she didn't care to be the source of unkind rumour. 'I wonder could there be something more serious at the bottom of it? Whether the Cudlums have got to a parting of the ways in any case?' She looked up thoughtfully. 'I've always had the sad feeling those two are not at all right for each other. There are no children, of course, so they're not bound together in that way. It's an odd thing to say, but I really can't picture Angela as the wife of a cathedral canon.'

'Other people have said that, Mummy,' said Caroline. 'But honestly I think it's mostly to do with her wanting to help over the church. And the Sunday Club. She started the club by herself. There's really no one else who'll rally people to the cause. Not the way she does. She's very charismatic.'

'Tch!' Tinder expostulated. 'That's a very overused word. And quite inappropriate when applied to such a silly woman.'

'I don't think she's silly at all, Daddy. I mean she could very likely win everyone over to her side, the way she was managing tonight.'

Tinder frowned. 'Is that what Peter Windle thought?'

'I believe so. He didn't seem happy about it, though. Did you know his company's involved in a development around here?'

'Of course I did,' he answered, too brusquely. 'That is . . . Did you actually ask him in tonight?'

'Sort of. Why?'

'Never mind.' Tinder stood up suddenly. 'Nigel Cudlum wasn't at this protest meeting?'

'No he wasn't, Daddy. And it wasn't exactly a protest—'

'I know exactly what it was.' He emptied his pipe into an ashtray. 'Look, I have to go out. Just remembered there's someone I promised to see.'

'At this time of night, dear?' asked Mrs Tinder.

'Yes. Shan't be long. Council business,' he said, then hurried from the room.

'Wear your over-shoes,' his wife called, but only a second before she heard the front door slam.

He always pleaded council business, and usually it suited her to accept the plea. Tonight his timing had been a little late to be credible, even to a wife as tolerant as Enid Tinder. That was why she felt there was more to it than what she chose to regard as his usual form of escapism. What Caroline had told them had seriously upset him – on top of his being on edge all day, a condition that was becoming more and more characteristic of him. Enid Tinder wished she knew what was troubling her husband, and her worried expression deepened as she went back to her knitting.

'What you mean is, you want to be on the winning side,' said Mia Frakraj. She was standing over the cooker in the kitchen of the flat at the other end of Kengrave Square.

'I didn't say that, my love. But Mrs Cudlum is very persuasive.'

'More persuasive than your wife, it seems?'

'That's not fair, Mia.'

'Yes it is. We are absolutely dependent on the church closing. Absolutely. But tonight you are giving a whole thousand pounds to keep it open. You must have known how I'd feel about that.'

He took another sip from the glass of water he was holding. He was sitting at the table, waiting for the supper she was cooking. They had been too busy in the store to have eaten before the meeting. 'If the church stays open, it will be a great victory for Mrs Cudlum and all the people who've supported her.'

'And you want to be one of those?'

'We both need to be, you and me.' He clasped and unclasped his hands around the glass. 'It wouldn't do to make enemies. Not here of all places. Not where we've made a very fine living, and expect to go on doing. Whatever happens. One way or the other.' He paused. 'Here we're accepted and respected. Totally. No silly troubles like we've had at Cordley.'

'So who's going to be your enemy because you don't give money to the church fund? You've given plenty to the church in the past. And played the organ without charge.' She stirred the pot briskly with a wooden ladle.

'Mr Jones the plumber's made enemies,' said her husband. 'It'll be bad for his trade. You'll see. And serve him right.'

'I don't believe Mr Jones cares. He won't need to either, not when he's sold his house for the development, like we're doing.'

'That's still up to providence, you know that.' He swallowed some more water. 'The Honourable Mrs Lodey will have taken notice of our gesture tonight.'

'Your gesture. And I don't believe she did notice.'

'Well I'm sure she did. She's a good customer.'

'For half a pound of tea once in a while. The Harrods van delivers groceries to her door every week.'

'She buys much more than tea from us. And Harrods stock many foods we don't. They're much bigger than us,' he added, as though that fact might not have been obvious. 'Anyway, I'm sure it's not only groceries they deliver to Kengrave House.'

'That's right. Wines and spirits too. We stock plenty of them.'

'Mrs Treasure made a very generous donation to the church. And she lives well outside the parish.' He was trying a different tack.

'Mrs Treasure is a successful actress, I understand, with a very wealthy husband. A gift of five thousand pounds doesn't mean nearly so much to them as one of one thousand pounds does to us.' She picked up the pan from the cooker and spooned a large helping of steaming rice and chicken onto a warm plate.

'It isn't a gift yet. Only a pledge. If the church goes, we'll keep the thousand.'

'That's what they call hedging the bet? Not quite as straightforward as we thought, then? I hope God is approving, Sundar. That's all I can say.'

His eyes showed she was onto his weakest spot. 'It's not like that at all. Well not so blatant as that. It's like Peter Windle explained at the meeting. They won't collect the pledges unless the Bishop cancels the redundancy notice.' He looked up from the plate she had put in front of him. 'Why aren't you eating then?'

'Because I'm not hungry. And because I still have some ticketing to do in the shop.'

'Not tonight, my love?'

'What's the difference? Tonight, or get up before six in the morning? I'd rather now. Enjoy your supper. I'll be back in half an hour. When you've finished, go and watch the end of the news with your mother. She likes that. It's nearly ten now.'

'More coffee, Mrs Treasure? It is decaffeinated. It won't keep you awake.'

'Thank you, Mrs Lodey. And I do wish you'd call me Molly.'

The old lady smiled. 'When we have known one another a trifle longer perhaps. Meantime, you must humour my old-fashioned whims. Or eccentricities. Oh dear, there *is* no more coffee. I'm so helpless when Modd isn't about.'

'Let me make some,' said Molly. 'I know where everything is. You'd like some more too, wouldn't you, Mark?'

'Please,' said her husband.

Before the offer could be refused by the hostess, Molly had whisked the silver pot from the tray and was on her way from the drawing room of Kengrave House to the kitchen below.

Miss Modd had excused herself shortly after the four had come in together after the meeting. Treasure, who had been driving the Rolls himself, had found a parking place outside the church when he and Molly had arrived for the meeting. Afterwards, because the melting snow would have made walking treacherous for Mrs Lodey, he had insisted on transporting the whole party the almost ludicrously short distance back to the house. The old lady had accepted the kindness on condition that the Treasures came in for refreshment.

'You'll take a little more whisky, Mr Treasure? Please help yourself.'

'Thank you. Only a spot.' He moved across to the drinks trolley.

'I'm sorry that both my guests are having to forage for themselves.'

'Don't be. But I hope Miss Modd is better in the morning.'

'It's so tiresome when she's indisposed, which isn't often. This time I fear she brought it upon herself. Over-indulgence at dinner last night. For so seemingly robust a woman, she has a quite fragile constitution.' Involuntarily, Mrs Lodey smoothed a delicate, ringed hand across her slim waist.

'But you're more robust than she, if you ate the same food.'

'Ah, that I didn't, although I was given the opportunity. Modd dined out last evening. As the guest of that importunate American. The one who spoke at the meeting.'

'Smurt?' Treasure was surprised at the information. 'And he asked you too?'

'In an informal manner. Through Modd, who is sometimes lax in her observation of the basic proprieties. It is not my habit to dine with total strangers.'

'I believe Smurt met Miss Modd when he called here yesterday morning.'

'Indeed.' It wasn't clear whether the single word was issued as question or confirmation. In either case, it was quite evident Mrs Lodey didn't care for Smurt.

'That was a very generous offer you made tonight.' The banker had resumed his seat, and taken the opportunity to broach the subject that was most on his mind.

'But you consider I was foolish to have made it?' Mrs Lodey looked hard at her guest.

'Not at all. It's your money. The cause is naturally very close to your heart.'

'I admit I acted largely on impulse. Otherwise I should have consulted you first.' The speaker dipped her head slightly as a due sign of penitence. 'Can I afford it?'

'Not really.' He gave a wry smile. 'If you had to cough up in earnest, it'd just about clean out your private portfolio.'

'I should still have my trust income.'

'Of course.'

'But in any case, you don't seem unduly alarmed at what I've done.'

'That's because I don't believe the Bishop is going to relent about closing the church. And even if he did so, on a temporary basis perhaps, to provide a breathing space, I don't think Mrs Cudlum is going to raise a hundred thousand pounds.'

'So that I cannot be asked for twice that sum? I see. I should still want the church to be repaired properly. That is, if it is allowed to remain open.'

Treasure looked more concerned than he had before. 'If anyone suggests you should provide more than the two-thirds you've promised, I would definitely expect you to ask my advice in advance, and to take it.'

'Now you're being stern with me, Mr Treasure.'

'I'm sorry.'

'Don't be. I quite like it.' This came with a distinctly coy smile and a girlish flutter of the eyelids.

'Like what, Mrs Lodey,' asked Molly returning with the coffee pot.

Mrs Lodey gave a guilty start, before quickly composing her features. 'Your husband is trying to prevent me from bankrupting myself. I appreciate his concern.'

'Will the church cost that much?' Molly resumed her seat as she was speaking.

Treasure got up to have his coffee cup filled, then wandered with it across to the end window. 'Repairing a dilapidated church can be a never-ending job financially.' He drew back a curtain a little. 'Doing one repair tends to reveal others. I must say, Saint Martin's looks more handsome under snow, and in the night light.'

'I am aware it is not a pretty church,' said Mrs Lodey resignedly.

'If it were, it'd probably be a lot easier to raise the money for repairs,' Molly put in.

'I've been thinking . . . ' Treasure paused for a moment,

intrigued by something he was watching through the window. 'I've been thinking,' he repeated, and still a touch preoccupied with what he saw going on outside. 'I'm sure your brother would want to make a contribution to the church.' A moment later he let the curtain close again, and returned to his seat. 'After all, Algernon Grenwood was Berty's grandfather too.'

Mrs Lodey returned an expression that might have been implying serious doubt over the last statement. 'Berty has never taken an interest in Saint Martin's,' she uttered almost hotly, before turning to Molly. 'It was kind of you to have offered so large a contribution tonight, my dear.'

'Sounds more than it'll cost after tax. If I pay by covenant,' said Molly glibly. 'In any case, I abhor small gestures, don't you?'

Treasure pouted. He was debating what the bank's clients Aziz Developments would say if they knew how much Mrs Lodey, the Chairman's sister, and Molly Treasure, the Chief Executive's wife, were doing to prevent their ever being able to build flats where the church now stood. Come to that, he doubted that the ladies' generosity had endeared the bank to Marvin Smurt either. While the last consideration didn't bother him at all, the other was beginning to make him just a touch uncomfortable.

'We can go back there now, Marlon. If you want,' said green-haired Kevin Hawker. 'It's on the way.'

'It'll be shut now,' Marlon Barclay replied, while having a final search through all his pockets.

'Anyway, we can 'ave a look going past.'

It was eleven-thirty. The two seventeen year olds had just split from the others in the group, outside a café they had all been to, a few hundred yards north of the church in Kengrave Road. Kevin and Marlon were the only ones who lived south from there.

Marlon had just discovered he had lost his clasp knife during the evening. It was the knife he used for his wood carving: wood carving was his hobby, and he was good at it.

'Come on then,' Marlon broke into a jog. The other followed. It was usually Marlon who took the lead. Their sneakers slapped against the wet slush on the pavement, echoing against the buildings in the nearly empty street.

When they had passed the west front of the church, they turned left into the top of Kengrave Square.

'There you are, see? Gate's not locked yet,' said Kevin, pushing the gate open and heading down the steps.

'Should be, prob'ly. There's no lights on below.'

The police patrol car seemed to appear from nowhere. It pulled onto the pavement behind the boys. 'What you two doing down there?' demanded the uniformed constable who'd jumped from the passenger seat as soon as the car stopped.

'We 'aven't been down there yet. We was just goin', wasn't we?' Marlon snapped back from where he had frozen between the second and third step. Kevin was about halfway down to the basement.

'Stand against the wall, then, lads,' ordered the policeman: his partner, now also alighted from the car, was standing just behind him.

'Why?' asked Marlon, who didn't like policemen.

'Because I want to shine my little light on the door down there, sonny, and you're in the flipping way,' answered the constable good-humouredly. He had come through the iron gate and was standing at the top of the steps. 'This gate open when you got here, was it?'

'Yeah,' said Marlon.

'We been in the church hall before this evenin',' Kevin called up. 'To a meetin'.'

'Is that so.' The first constable extinguished the beam of light he'd been playing on the area at the bottom. He exchanged a look over his shoulder with his partner, who took his place at the top of the steps. 'Stay where you are then, lads,' ordered the first constable as he clattered down the steps past the two.

When he got near the bottom, the constable turned on his torch again and squatted beside what from above had looked like a bundle of clothes splayed over the lowest steps. Now the bundle was revealed as the inert body of a woman. She was lying face downwards, neck bent at an unnatural angle, the clothing around the neck saturated with blood.

Careful about what he touched, the constable was trying for a pulse at the woman's wrist.

'Ambulance, Charlie,' he called up to his partner, 'but I think she's a goner.' His light caught the glint of something in the woman's right hand. The right arm was half extended. The object in the hand was an open clasp knife.

' 'Ey, that's my knife. Lost it in there tonight.' This was Marlon, who despite orders had pushed past Kevin and was standing only a step above the hand.

'I told you to stay where you were,' said the policeman, angrily. But when he looked up he could see the boy was transfixed, mouth open and aghast. 'What you know about this, lad?'

'I don't know nothin'. Nothin' except who she is.'

'Who is she, then?'

But it was Kevin who answered, from immediately behind Marlon. 'Chrise, it's Mrs Cudlum,' he said. 'Mrs Cudlum, the Vicar's wife.'

Chapter Ten

Treasure put back the kitchen telephone and returned to the breakfast table, shaking his head. 'That was Miss Modd. There's been the most terrible accident.'

'So I gathered,' said Molly. 'Mrs Cudlum. She's dead?'

'I'm afraid so. Last night.'

'How?'

'You remember the church porch? With the basement entrance immediately underneath? Well some heavy slates came away from the porch roof while Mrs Cudlum was going up the steps. One of them hit her in the back of the neck. Seems it severed an artery. She was dead when they found her.'

'How absolutely ghastly. But how could a slate— ?'

'All too easily, I'm afraid. The main church roof is known to be unsafe. Slates have been falling off it for some time. But they've been caught by the parapets. So it wasn't considered a danger to the public. Nobody seems to have thought about the porch roof. It has a gutter, which I suppose might have stopped a slate, but that's come away too. Must have had something to do with the weight of the snow, followed by that fast thaw.'

'When did Miss Modd hear?'

'At midnight. The local police were round at Kengrave House.'

'What? Knocking them up at that time?'

'There were lights on still. Mrs Lodey was up. They went there, and to the Tinders' house next door.'

'Of course, Mrs Tinder is the churchwarden. Miss Modd

111

mentioned that on Sunday. She wasn't at the meeting though. Something to do with Mr Tinder not approving.'

'Well the police wanted to talk to someone who'd been at the meeting. To find out what time it ended.'

'What time did it end? I can't remember.' Molly poured herself more coffee.

'I thought around half past nine. Miss Modd said the same.'

'When did they find Mrs Cudlum?'

'At half past eleven. Or soon after.'

'So she was lying there for over two hours?'

'They think not that long. D'you remember Mrs Lodey had a word with her at the end? While we were talking to the Tinder daughter and her boyfriend— '

'Peter Windle. Yes, I remember.'

'Well she told them she was staying on to do some more work on the word processor. It's in the office down there.'

'But wasn't anyone with her?'

'Possibly. I've no idea. Couldn't have been at the end. When she left. So I suppose she could have been lying there quite a long time.'

'Would she have died quickly? I mean— ' Molly broke off with a shudder.

'The chances are, very quickly.'

'What about her husband? He wasn't at the meeting.'

'He was giving a lecture somewhere. But he was home about ten, apparently.'

'So didn't he wonder where his wife was?'

Treasure shrugged. 'According to what the police told Miss Modd, he was reading in his study when they came round with the bad news.'

'So he hadn't gone looking for her?'

'Perhaps he thought the meeting was still going on.'

'Hardly.' She looked doubtful. 'Well, perhaps. Or perhaps he thought she'd come in and gone to bed. Must have been a terrible shock.'

'He took it very well, the police said. Miss Modd offered to go round to him but they didn't think it necessary. Did you know she'd been trained as a nurse?'

'No.' Molly stroked the end of her nose, a certain sign of true perplexity. 'I wonder why Mrs Cudlum was leaving the basement that way?'

'Why shouldn't she?'

'Because there's a way there from the vicarage. Don't you remember? That nice Mr Frakraj pointed out the door on Sunday.'

'Yes, I remember. Perhaps she had to lock up on the other side.'

'She could have done that from the inside surely?'

'There's a gate into the street. At the top of the basement steps. Maybe that has to be locked.' He extended his look of speculation to his coffee cup. 'Is there any more milk?'

'Mmm.' Molly reached into the fridge behind her. 'Poor Mrs Cudlum. I hope she didn't suffer. Wasn't it Mrs Frakraj who asked what would happen if the roof fell in? That was morbidly prescient of her, wasn't it?'

'Yes. And it was Mrs Cudlum said the insurance would pay. Now they'll be paying out on her own life.'

Molly refilled the milk jug from the carton in her hand. 'Will that be a lot of money?'

'Depends on what the policy says. And whether the Vicar's lawyers advise him to go for more than he's offered. Whatever he gets is bound to be fairly substantial.'

'Because it's negligence by the church?'

'Well, the church surveyors. Or the insurance company's surveyors. Difficult to allocate direct blame, of course. I suppose the porch roof could have held up for ages except under freakish weather conditions. And the chance of someone being directly under a falling slate would be pretty remote.' Treasure was non-executive chairman of the Regal Sun Assurance Company – happily not the insurers of St Martin's Church, a fact he had purposely checked at the end of the meeting the night before.

'Spotty Nottel, the one who took the minutes last night, the parish treasurer,' Molly began. 'Didn't he say the insurance company had given notice they weren't going to renew the policy? Not unless things were put right?'

'Yes. Pity they hadn't acted sooner.'

'For Mrs Cudlum's sake. One doesn't think of lives being at risk when it comes to that sort of insurance. Though I suppose one should.' She sighed. 'Terrible loss for the Vicar.'

'I expect so.'

'What d'you mean expect?' Molly's eyebrows raised.

'Only that it seemed to me she was leaving him.'

'Nonsense. They were probably devoted. She was just going to hang on in London till the church was saved.'

'Or so it might be interpreted by an incorrigible romantic like you, darling. From my impression of the two of them on Sunday, I wouldn't have thought they were made for each other.'

'Because he talks a bit plummy and she's ripe regional?'

He shook his head. 'Nothing so trivial. I got a strong feeling he was the ambitious type.'

'And that she wasn't?'

'Quite the opposite. He's aggressive too. She looked the sort who'd suffer a husband of that kind till she reached breaking-point.'

'After which she'd go mad? Or go her own way, you mean?'

'I think so.'

'And the Salchester move was the breaking-point?'

'Anathema for her, I'd say. But the chance of saving Saint Martin's was possibly a marvellous excuse for staying put. And staying sane.'

'What brought on all this analysis?'

'I was deeply bored by the sermon on Sunday.'

'Ooo!' Molly exclaimed accusingly. 'And you said at Mrs Lodey's you found it learned, or something of the sort. You are a fraud.'

'He went on too long, that's all. Before the end, my fertile mind turned to speculating about the preacher.' He took the last, and cold piece of toast from the rack. 'I felt sorry for Mrs Cudlum when we first met, but she was obviously in her element last night. D'you remember, she announced that decision to stay as though it were an ode to victory?'

'Who d'you think will take on the church appeal? It'll be quite a challenge.'

'My guess is no one. There'll be pious noises but no further action.'

'I don't believe that.'

'You're being romantic again. The church isn't destined to become a monument to the martyred Mrs Cudlum.' He spread marmalade on the dry toast as he spoke. 'Most of the activists there last night were also realists. Even the ones who wanted to keep the church open. They know that raising a hundred thousand is a pipe dream.'

'But they got over twelve thousand right then and there.'

'And that was the easy bit. Because everyone interested in saving the church was at the meeting. A lot of them will have had second thoughts this morning. The accident will get them off the hook.'

'My offer stands,' said Molly stoutly.

'You're special, darling. I've always believed that.'

She blew him a kiss before saying: 'So who's going to be unhooked? Not Mrs Lodey?'

'Hmm. I'm not sure. Miss Modd— '

'Miss Modd didn't pledge anything.'

'She didn't have to. As a likely beneficiary when Mrs Lodey expires, her future was affected by the old lady's promise.'

'Oh yes, of course. And Mr Frakraj?'

'Has a very saleable lease he's waiting to trade for a new shop, according to Miss Modd.'

'But he gave a thousand pounds.'

'And nearly gave his wife apoplexy. Didn't you hear them behind us?'

'What about the American evangelist?'

'Smurt? He's in a different category. The appeal's only one of several barriers to his progress, or lack of it.' Treasure shook his head. 'He's really very second rate. If his organisation is so red-hot, I wonder why they sent such a blunderer on a really quite sensitive mission.'

'You snubbed him pretty badly when he tried to get your support.'

'And he richly deserved it. Still, he'll be delighted if the appeal's abandoned. So will young Windle incidentally.'

'He didn't pledge anything. But he was terribly helpful with that advice he gave.'

'Which was very much in his own company's interest.'

'Which company?'

'He's one of Aziz Developments' bright young accountants.'

'Who are they?'

He told her.

'The accident could have been a sign from God, would you say, Sundar?' asked Mia Frakraj.

'What d'you mean by that?'

'That God decided Mrs Cudlum's campaign to save the church wasn't to be.'

'No, no. That's sacrilegious talk,' her husband replied, but in a way hoping she might be right.

'But I can't be sacrilegious. I'm agnostic. That's why I am asking you.'

Frakraj had to think for a moment.

They were alone in the Kengrave Road store. She was setting up the tills at the two check-outs. He was restocking the impulse-purchase points near by. It was ten to eight, forty minutes before opening time. The other three members of staff would not be arriving until eight-fifteen.

'You liked Mrs Cudlum,' said Frakraj in the despondent tone that had coloured his speech and manner today, from even before they had heard the news of the accident.

116

'Everybody liked her,' she replied carefully. 'Doesn't mean I liked what she was doing. I'm glad the campaign will be over now. It's an ill wind that blows nobody any good. That's what they say, isn't it?' She moved across the aisle to the other till.

'You think the campaign will stop?'

'Of course it will. You know that too.'

They both looked round when they heard the rattling of the door-handle. 'Not open yet,' Frakraj mimed, shaking his head at the figure outside, before he recognised who it was.

'It's Emrys Jones,' said Mia, going to the door, and opening it. 'Come in, Emrys.'

The Welsh plumber hurried over the threshold. '*Duw, Duw*, it's cold again. 'Morning both. You've heard about Mrs Cudlum, of course? Thought you must have. Terrible isn't it? Fine woman. Real tragedy.' He waited an obsequial moment – but only one – before continuing. 'Ought to strengthen us all to what has to be done. Straightaway. No messin' about.'

'What is that, Emrys?' Mia enquired, adjusting the sari around her head.

'Why, insist that the church is closed. Barricaded up as a public menace. That's until they can demolish it. Before it claims any more innocent lives.' He got extra emotive value from a prolonged 'innocent'.

Frakraj shook his head. 'I don't think the authorities will agree to that.' He didn't like Jones, and more especially he didn't like the lascivious looks Jones was always giving Mia.

'Well, we'll have to make them agree, won't we? That's democracy, for you.'

'It was only a few tiles that fell.'

'With devastating results, though. Devastating,' Jones thundered, while looking to Mia for support.

'Emrys is right, Sundar,' she said.

'But the restoration appeal fund could mean— ' began Frakraj.

'What restoration appeal fund?' the other man cut in. 'Dead as . . . I mean, over and done with, that is. Mrs Cudlum was the beginning and the end of it. Worthy woman, as I've said already, but totally misguided over that.'

'Many people may still be ready to give,' said Frakraj, but with conviction definitely waning.

'Sundar pledged a thousand pounds,' Mia offered in a tone that was critical and with a look that was apologetic.

'I know. Because he's a compassionate man, moved on the instant by a spiritual appeal. But you regretted it after, Sundar? I'll bet you did.'

Sundar looked even more dejected than before. 'Later on I did think perhaps . . . '

'Of course. Was that why you went back to see Mrs Cudlum, I wonder?'

There was silence for a second. Then Mia said: 'You went back, Sundar? When was that?'

'I didn't go back.'

'Sorry, I was sure I'd seen you from my bedroom window. By the basement gate. Around quarter past ten was it?' said Jones. It was more a statement than a question.

'I went out to get some fresh air. After supper. I wasn't going back. Just passing.'

'You didn't tell me, Sundar,' complained his wife. 'You could have been helping me down here with the ticketing.'

'I wasn't out long. I needed to think.'

'Understandable that was,' offered Jones, assuming the rôle of condemned prisoner's friend. 'Bothered in your mind about all that money you'd pledged. Letting your friends down. Letting Mia down. When we all have so much at stake.'

Frakraj opened his mouth as if to protest, but it was Jones who spoke again, ahead of him.

'Any road, I reckon all bets are off after Mrs Cudlum's tragic death,' said the plumber. 'Never be a better chance to get the church closed, once and for all. Ought to be a cinch. Only we've got to watch out for that looney American. The tall one. Name like Dirt.'

'Smurt,' said Mia.

'That's it. Did you hear him on the radio news just now? The LBC news?'

The others shook their heads. 'Talking about the accident?' asked Frakraj.

'Saying just what we should be saying. At the start that was. That the church is unsafe. Beyond saving as things stand.'

'Well that's good isn't it?' Mia asked.

'Not when he went on that these Investors for Jesus could make the building safe. Safe for fresh Christian work. His words, not mine, mark you. No, it wasn't right. It wasn't even consistent. The place is a menace. Mark my words, he only wants it for the site.' Jones blew his nose. 'And Smurt went back to the basement last night. Definitely.' He was eyeing Frakraj as he emphasised the last word.

'After the meeting?' This was Frakraj.

'Yes. I saw him. Before I saw you. Before I thought I saw you, that is,' he corrected. 'Probably out to make a deal with Mrs Cudlum. Poor soul. Well, I must be on my way. Plenty of work for plumbers today. Treacherous weather. Got your pipes lagged, I hope.'

'I'm afraid I listen to the BBC news, Bishop,' said the Archdeacon into the telephone, defensively, as though listening to anything except the BBC was in some way un-Anglican.

'And I had an early service,' the Bishop replied. 'I just got back. My wife heard it. Poor woman was knocked on the head by a slate.'

'Good gracious, not— '

'No, not my wife. Mrs Cudlum, the Vicar's wife. Killed instantly. Terrible thing. Then there was some American evangelist describing the church as a death trap.'

'We know it's been in poor repair for some time, Bishop.'

'But not a death trap?'

'Certain precautions have been taken, I'm sure. Of course, the dilapidated state of the fabric was basically the reason we've gone for redundancy.'

'Well the sooner it's done with the better. Have the Church Commissioners accepted the recommendation for redundancy?'

'What is termed due process is being applied.'

'Damn due process,' said the Bishop. 'That's not fast enough. You must hurry up the lawyers. And another thing. Any more publicity must come from us. As soon as I have the full facts, I'll be available for interview. You can tell everybody that. It's not something we should shirk. Or need to. We've plenty of good spokesmen.' It was some time since he'd been asked to do the 'Thought for the Day' spot on morning radio. 'Our recommendation for making Saint Martin's redundant is clear and unequivocal.' He paused. 'It is isn't it?'

'We haven't said the church should be knocked down, Bishop.'

'Well we should now. I clearly remember we decided it was pastorally superfluous, and of no aesthetic or historic value. How much is the site worth?'

'I've no idea, Bishop.'

'Well can you find out? Discreetly of course. My wife said this American wants to buy it.'

'I hardly think—'

'Neither do I, but we should be informed on all the options.'

'I believe there have already been overtures from a development company. Through the Church Commissioners.'

'Good. The more the merrier.'

The Archdeacon sighed, but not audibly. 'Should I write to Nigel Cudlum on your behalf, Bishop?'

'Nigel who? Oh! Oh no. I'll do that. Right away.' The Bishop cleared his throat. 'Thanks for reminding me.'

Chapter Eleven

'Detective Inspector Daynon,' announced Miss Gaunt, holding the door into Treasure's office wide open. It was Friday mid-morning, and the eighth day since Mrs Cudlum's death.

'Good morning, Mr Treasure. Sorry to impose at short notice. Thank you for seeing me.'

'Not at all. So how can I help you?' said the banker as the two shook hands.

Daynon was in his early thirties, medium height and thickset, with the springy movements of a boxer. His black hair was short but well styled. The dark eyes, below straight, thick brows, were busy and intelligent; the mouth drooped at the edges; the jaw was square. His speaking voice was low-pitched, and the words clipped, with just a touch of East London in the intonation. The first impression was of a businesslike man who probably didn't laugh a lot. He was dressed in a neat, single-breasted grey flannel suit, a white shirt and a sobre, red-patterned tie.

'It's about the death of Mrs Angela Elizabeth Cudlum,' he said, taking the seat Treasure had indicated at the round table.

'So you mentioned to my secretary,' said Treasure, sitting two chairs away from the visitor. 'Very sad business. We were at the meeting the night she died. But perhaps you know that? My wife was at the funeral on Tuesday.'

'I've just come from the inquest, sir.'

'Ah, I gather it was adjourned from Monday. Didn't hold up the funeral, though. So what was the verdict? Accident I suppose?'

'No. Murder. By a person or persons unknown. The jury was unanimous.' The policeman was studying the other's reaction to these sharply delivered intelligences.

'You surprise me.' Treasure rubbed a cheek with the tips of his fingers. 'In fact, you astonish me. I understood the deodand was a falling slate.'

'The what?'

'The deodand. The object deemed by its movement to have been the cause of a death by misadventure. Sorry, my Uncle John was a coroner. Please go on.'

'Deodand. Very interesting.' Daynon gave an energetic nod before continuing. 'The murder weapon was a slate all right. But it didn't fall on her. Someone slammed it into the back of her neck. Very hard. From behind.'

'Like a rabbit punch?'

'Yes, but worse than that. The impact would probably have killed her anyway. But both vertebral arteries were severed as well.'

'Which would mean a pretty quick death?'

'That's right. Looked at clinically, it was an accurate job with an unwieldy implement. The forensic reports were very straightforward and specific.'

'I see. I gather she had an open knife in her hand. Is that significant?'

'We don't know for sure. Not yet. But it's possible she was using it to defend herself.'

'So now you're looking for a murderer?'

'But not here, sir,' the other offered promptly with a twitch of a smile, and eyes continuing overtly to docket all Treasure's responses. 'Mrs Cudlum died at between ten-nineteen and ten-twenty-two. I understand you and your wife were with Mrs Monica Lodey at Kengrave House at that time?'

'Yes. Let's see . . . Yes, as far as I remember from about

nine forty-five to ten-thirty. Or perhaps a few minutes after ten-thirty.'

'That fits with what Mrs Lodey told us. I expect your wife will confirm it.' He had taken a small notebook from a side pocket, and was rifling through the pages when he stopped and looked up. 'Marvellous acting talent your wife has.' This had been offered as simple fact, not unctuous compliment. He looked down again immediately.

'Thank you. I'll be sure to tell her you said that. As a matter of fact, she's not awfully good at remembering times. Curious that. She never forgets a line on stage.' He paused. 'Mrs Lodey is a remarkable old lady, of course.' Suddenly he felt a stab of guilt because there had been a message for him to telephone Mrs Lodey, and he hadn't done so yet: she had called him earlier when he had been in a meeting.

'And Miss Modd, Mrs Lodey's companion, she was in the house too at the time, sir?'

'She came back with us. From the meeting.' His hesitation in replying had been momentary; he had probably only imagined it had registered in the inspector's expression. 'Then she excused herself because she wasn't well. Can you tell me how you have the time of death so accurately? There wasn't a witness was there?'

'Only the murderer,' said Daynon dully. 'But there were two witnesses to when she'd last eaten. At seven-ten. Given that, forensic can pinpoint the time of death to within two or three minutes. No question. From an analysis of stomach content. The body temperature suggested death could have been fifteen minutes earlier. But the weather was playing tricks that night. In any case, the stomach evidence is completely reliable.'

'Yes, I think I've heard that before. So. The slates from the porch were dislodged on purpose?'

'No. The weather brought them down. Three of them. After the gutter had swung loose. They fell straight into the area below. Right outside the door to the basement.'

'You'd have thought they'd have broken up on impact.'

'Two of them did. At least, they broke in half. The third, the one the murderer used, that stayed intact. It had a very sharp edge. Worn down by exposure probably.'

'Did that one land in snow?'

The policeman nodded. 'That's one of the theories. Thing is, they would all have fallen straight down. We tested with other slates. Mrs Cudlum would have been in the wrong position.'

'To be hit by any of them?'

'In the way she was hit. In the neck. Accidentally that is. She'd have been too upright. That's what made us suspicious. Even before the medical reports.'

'Because the angle of the blow was wrong?'

'Dead wrong. On top of that, forensic showed there was a second thrust behind it. The extra shove, as she was falling, it pressed the edge further home. Broke part of it. That's what confirmed it was murder not accident.' Daynon lunged back in his seat.

'What a terrible thing. So whoever did it must have been waiting for her in the shadows down there?'

The inspector looked dubious. 'Possibly. It's quite a small space, of course. Not much chance of conceal-ment.'

'And I seem to remember a light over the basement door.'

'There is one, but it was out when the body was found. So far, we've assumed it was turned out by Mrs Cudlum. When she was leaving. Or maybe by someone who left with her.'

Treasure's eyebrows lifted. 'The murderer you mean? That it was someone who came out of the basement with her?'

'Behind her probably. Someone with a key who locked the door. Either that, or someone took Mrs Cudlum's key. There was no key on the body, but the door was locked.'

'Slammed to, perhaps?'

'No. It's a mortice lock.'

Treasure let out a breath slowly. 'So the chances are it was someone she knew? Gets worse, doesn't it? Incidentally, my wife wondered why she came out that way at all. There's direct access to the church and the basement from the vicarage.'

'She had to lock the street gate. It was her responsibility to lock up all round, because the hall was booked in her name.'

'We thought that gate might have been the reason. Oh, thank you, Miss Gaunt. You'll have some coffee, Inspector?'

Miss Gaunt had entered with a tray of coffee things and a plate of chocolate biscuits. She put these beside Treasure, and a folded note in front of him. 'Shall I pour?' she asked.

'No, we'll manage, thanks,' said her employer.

Miss Gaunt left the room as circumspectly as she had entered it.

'No milk, one sugar, thank you,' said Daynon a moment later, in staccato response to an enquiry from Treasure.

'I suppose there were no footprints?' asked the banker, pushing a cup along the table, and pocketing the note he had just read. It was an urgent request to call Jumbo Crib-Cranton – possibly because the verdict of the Cudlum inquest had been promulgated to St James's Square.

'Not usable footprints, sir. Not by the time we got there. The snow had stopped, and the thaw had started before the meeting ended. Around seventy people left by those steps. We're sorting through the detritus. Not at all profitable. Except for a pound coin we found. Oh, thanks.' He helped himself to one, and then to two biscuits from the proffered plate.

'What about fingerprints?'

'Some. On the railings to the steps. From the few people at the meeting who weren't wearing gloves. The murderer wasn't one of them.'

'How d'you know that?'

'The tile used in the killing was clean as a whistle.'

Treasure stirred his coffee. 'So tell me why you've come to me? Not just to confirm we were at Kengrave House at the time of the crime? Though, in a way, I'm quite glad we were.'

'That was my first reason, sir. More than that, I need to know if you saw anyone as you left Mrs Lodey's that night? In Kengrave Square?'

'That's just what I've been asking myself. So far the answer's no. And I distinctly recall the square being empty. My wife and I both remarked on it. It wasn't that late, of course. We thought the weather was keeping people at home. Except those who'd been to the meeting, and they'd long since dispersed, of course.'

'And you drove out of the square by the west side?'

'Yes. Past the church, then turned left into Kengrave Road. There was still a bit of activity there, as you'd expect. Oh, and the two Indian restaurants at the end of the square, the ones opposite the church porch, they were open when we went past.' He paused and grimaced. 'I'm sorry, none of that's much use to you, is it?'

'Can't be helped, sir.' The policeman shifted in his seat. 'Oh, don't mind if I do. Thanks.' He accepted another biscuit and bit into it. 'There is another area where you may be able to assist. We're naturally trying to establish the motive for the crime. It seems that could possibly lie in what was to happen to the church.'

'Possibly, as you say. But I doubt it, even so,' said Treasure with decision.

'But there's been a good deal of controversy over whether it should be closed. Mrs Cudlum was campaigning to keep it open. And by all accounts she was winning. So she was working against the interests of a lot of people. People whose futures depended on what happened to the building. Or the site. People and organisations.'

Treasure pouted out his lips before replying. 'Redundancy's been proposed for the church. But even if that

126

goes through, I'd have thought it'd be a long time before there's any decision on what would happen to the church, let alone the site. These things take time.'

'Our information is, the building's in such a bad state, the authorities are ready to hurry the procedures. In any case, time wouldn't have to be the key, would it?'

'For anyone prepared to murder Mrs Cudlum to improve the chances of redundancy and demolition?' The banker shook his head. 'I find that concept difficult to credit, Inspector. If the church does go, I suppose the ultimate major beneficiary will be whoever buys the site. And really, I don't believe property companies arrange murder for corporate gain. And a notional gain at best. The idea's absurd.'

Daynon gave what might have been an involuntary glance around the expensively furnished office as he replied. 'Perhaps some individual in such a company would see a big enough personal incentive? We understand Aziz Developments are pretty certain to get the site. They already own the freeholds and the leases of most of the smaller sites around it. Or else they have arrangements to acquire them at the right time. So they could block anyone else—'

'Aziz Developments are customers of Grenwood, Phipps,' the banker interrupted. 'You won't expect me to comment on their affairs?'

'Not if you don't want to, sir.'

Treasure chuckled. 'Well, I don't. Only to say it's unlikely they'd be the only people after the place in an open-market sale. And since it's church property, I'm pretty sure it would have to be an open-market sale.' And he still tended to this belief, despite what Gerald Head had told him. 'There could possibly be restrictions on certain types of buyers, I suppose,' he added.

'Moral restrictions?'

'More religious, I'd have thought. But moral too, perhaps. And as to your hypothesis about Aziz owning surrounding sites, even if it's true, it certainly doesn't mean they'd be the only ones in the running to get the main site. The church and the buildings immediately attached to it make a viable development area on their own. That's without the smaller bits on either side.'

'Some of those little sites, private houses and shops they are mostly, they're only promised to Aziz Developments, of course.'

'Is that so? I honestly don't know.'

'Oh yes, sir. There's no secret about that. Or if there was, there isn't any more. A lot of those owners just might be ready to commit a crime to make sure the deal goes through. That would make a more human motive, wouldn't you think?'

'For murder? Only marginally less unlikely than having company directors doing people in to help with the cash flow.'

The Detective Inspector met the drollery with a cool, polite smile. 'You know Mr Frakraj, I believe?'

'The organist?' Treasure responded carefully. 'Yes. Nice man.'

'He owns a fourteen-year lease on his shop and the flat above it, next to the church. That's part of the viable site you mentioned. The freehold of the shop site is already owned by Aziz Developments. They've offered him a very attractive proposition over the lease, but it's dependent on their getting the church site too.'

'Really, Inspector, I don't think I can go on discussing Aziz Developments' affairs unless— '

'Just Mr Frakraj, sir. Not Aziz,' the other interrupted hastily but with stolid persistence. 'We know he offered a thousand pounds toward Mrs Cudlum's fund.'

'Yes. I heard him do it.'

'Wouldn't you say that was an odd thing for someone to do who stands to make more than most people, if the church is destroyed? Buying out that fourteen-year lease is going to be essential for whoever gets the church site.'

'Mmm. That's probably right, but I don't see— '

'Since you were there, sir, would you say that the thousand pounds he donated might have been a diversion on his part?'

'Prior to his doing in Mrs Cudlum? No, I don't. I agree it was inconsistent.'

'Or an impulsive gesture that he regretted so bitterly afterwards that he had to atone for it? Drastically.'

'But Frakraj doesn't seem in the least like a murderer.' As soon as he'd spoken, Treasure wished he hadn't come out with anything so ill considered. It was a sure sign that the policeman was beginning to irritate him.

'Not every impulsive murderer looks the part, sir.'

Treasure leaned back, his hands on the table. 'I see your line of argument. Why do you think this was a murder done on impulse?'

'The weapon, sir. The weapon almost certainly points to that.'

'So?'

'Have you spoken to Mr Frakraj since Mrs Cudlum's death by any chance?'

'No.'

'Or had any form of communication with him? Directly, or indirectly through anyone else?'

'No I haven't.'

'And are you quite sure you didn't see Mr Frakraj as you left the square? Please think very carefully.'

'I've told you already, I didn't see anyone. Why d'you ask about Frakraj particularly?'

Daynon flipped a page of his notebook. 'Because he says he left his flat to walk in the square at ten-twenty, was there for ten minutes, and didn't pass the church till the end. He also claims he saw you, and that you probably saw him. Actually he saw your car leaving. There's someone else who claims to have seen him near the church porch, but not at the time Mr Frakraj says he was there.'

'Earlier or later?' Treasure asked slowly.

The policeman looked up from the notebook. 'Earlier,

I'm afraid. But not much earlier. Around ten-fifteen.'

'I see. Pity I didn't see him. But if he killed Mrs Cudlum at say ten-twenty, it's hardly likely he'd have been dithering about in the square ten minutes later, is it?'

'Possibly not, sir.'

'And there's still the chance my wife saw him, of course.'

'Perhaps, but not if you both remarked at the time that there was no one in the square, sir. Anyway, we should have Mrs Treasure's answer on that by now. As I was leaving the station, one of my officers was making an appointment to see her in Cheyne Walk.' He watched as the banker's face clouded. 'Perhaps I should have mentioned that before. You understand, we needed you to answer separately. The question was very important. For Mr Frakraj.'

'We shouldn't have colluded to give you false information if you'd seen us together, Inspector.'

'Of course not, sir.'

Treasure looked at the time. 'Well, if all you really needed was—' he had begun stiffly.

'Just one other small point, sir. I believe you know Mr Marvin Smurt? Of the Community of Investors for Jesus?'

'Yes. He came to see me here last week. I also saw him at the church meeting. But not to speak to.'

'He's not a customer of this bank, sir?'

Treasure was silent for a second. 'No. He was hoping we might be able to act for his organisation, but after some consideration we had to decline. I told him as much on the telephone last Monday.'

'Is it possible you could tell me the reason for turning him down, sir.'

'There could have been a conflict of interest with another customer.'

'Thank you. There was no other reason, sir? A less savoury one?'

'No. But even if there had been, it's unlikely I'd be volunteering it,' the banker answered more sternly.

'Quite so, sir. Professional ethics, and so on. And it's no use asking if you saw Mr Smurt in Kengrave Square as you were leaving that night?'

'Not really, since I keep telling you we saw no one at all. Was he supposed to have been there?'

'Yes. But not at the time you were leaving. He went back to the church after the meeting. He says, at five to ten. To speak to Mrs Cudlum. Claims he was trying to persuade her to drop her campaign and join his.' Daynon jerked on his brief reflex smile again before continuing. 'So far as we know, he's the last person to have seen her alive.'

'And did he succeed in persuading her?'

'Seems not. According to him, she sent him off with a flea in his ear.'

'What time did he leave her?'

'He says at exactly ten o'clock.'

'And was she alone when he left?'

'He says so, yes. He went on to a pub called the Bell and Hammer where he had an appointment at ten. He was there all right. Till ten-sixteen. Is there any reason for your asking, sir?'

Treasure shrugged. 'Just curiosity.'

'The person Mr Smurt was meeting was a lady. She didn't show up, but the barmaid remembers him.'

'People do. Because of his height.'

'I expect so. The lady was Miss Modd. As you said, she was poorly and retired early.'

'Indeed,' Treasure answered, and without further commitment.

Chapter Twelve

Miss Modd was at her heartiest when she opened the door. 'Of course, we knew you'd be calling, Mr Treasure. Your secretary telephoned. Said you'd be here around six-thirty. So you're spot on. Mrs Lodey's upstairs in the drawing room. I'm afraid the Vicar's there too. With Lancelot Tinder from next door. But it's high time they were both moved on.'

The last observations were delivered with the same gusto as the rest, so Treasure hoped they were no more decipherable to the people upstairs than the murmur of the conversation from there was to the two of them here in the hall.

'I don't need to see Mrs Lodey for long. I'm just delivering some papers for her. They happened to come on my desk as I was leaving the bank.'

'Must make you the highest-paid delivery service in the business, Mr Treasure.'

'Not if you know the price of delivering gold bullion these days,' the banker responded dourly. 'Look, could you and I have a private word? Before we go up?' It was Miss Modd he had really come to see: Mrs Lodey being engaged was proving providential.

'Naturally. Let's use the morning room. Would your chauffeur like to come in for a cuppa in the kitchen?'

'I shouldn't think so. I really won't be here that long.'

The morning room was nearly square and of modest size, with one Venetian window facing east. It was sparsely furnished. An extremely small and quite elderly television receiver stood in front of the blocked-off fire-place. Two very upright wooden armchairs of extreme utilitarian design faced the television screen, offering, in their unyielding shape, a kind of puritan discouragement to overlong viewing.

There were scatter rugs on the polished wood floor, with a mahogany card table covered with a velvet cloth planted on one of these, and set slightly off the centre of the room. Four small, matching upholstered chairs with wooden arms were arranged around the table, in appearance more inviting than the others, but only marginally so. The lighting, from wall-brackets, was poor. It gave small opportunity to gauge whether the pictures on display, mostly prints, were better than the somewhat haphazard order of their hanging otherwise suggested.

There was only one radiator, which is what Treasure would have anticipated, except he would have preferred that it had been turned on. Miss Modd, dressed in heavy tweeds overall, seemed not to notice the drop in temperature when they entered from the hall.

Altogether it was a room given over to transitory and less noble pleasures, but with minimum enticement.

'Take a pew,' urged Miss Modd, pulling out one of the chairs from the table. Brusquely she pushed aside the half-finished game of patience spread on the table top.

'Game not coming out?' Treasure asked, seating himself opposite.

'Not mine. Mrs Lodey's. She never comes back to a game she leaves. Strong pointer to a character trait in that, wouldn't you say?'

'Probably.' Treasure cleared his throat. 'You possibly know I had a visit this morning from a detective inspector?' he went on abruptly, but anxious to get through a difficult confrontation.

'Yes. That man Daynon. Mrs Lodey told me after you rang her back. He's been here too. Sly bugger, I thought.'

She squared her shoulders. 'Has his job to do though, I suppose.'

'He was checking on all our movements after the church meeting.'

'I know. Working on the assumption Angela Cudlum was done in by an interested local party. Someone connected with Saint Martin's. I told him, if you believe that, you'll believe anything.'

'So you think it was an outsider?'

'Obviously. One of those punks. Someone on drugs out to steal the price of a fix. The streets just aren't safe any more.'

'That's a possibility, I suppose,' said Treasure, while thinking it less than that. 'I hadn't heard she was robbed.'

'She wasn't raped either, thank God,' Miss Modd offered inconsequentially.

'Daynon said you were in the house after the meeting. I confirmed that you came back with us. He also said you'd had an appointment with Smurt at the Bell and Hammer, but hadn't kept it because you hadn't felt well enough to go out.'

'Quite right.'

'Was it?'

'How d'you mean?'

'I happened to be looking out of the drawing-room window upstairs at about twenty past ten. I saw you coming back here. Through the gate from Kengrave Square gardens opposite. You were relocking the gate.'

Miss Modd's eyebrows moved up and down several times, creasing and uncreasing her forehead in evident inward agitation. 'I could deny that, of course.' She folded her hands in her lap. 'I shan't though. Yes, I went out again that night. To meet Marvin Smurt. We'd had a quick word when the meeting ended. Arranged to meet at the Six Bells. Silly ass got the pub wrong. Went to the Bell and Hammer. They're both in Kengrave Road. I was late. The Six Bells was totally empty when I got there. I thought he'd given me up, so I didn't stay. No one saw me. The barmaid had her back turned.'

'And no one saw you going or coming back?'

'No one except you, it seems. I used the gardens for that reason. And Kengrave Place. It was an awkward time for me to be out.'

'The murder— '

'The murder's made it more so since, of course,' she interrupted. 'Usually at that time of night, I'm supposed to be dancing attendance on Mrs Lodey. Especially if we've got visitors. You and your lady wife were here, of course. I'd been out late the night before, too. It was why I pretended to be under the weather. So that I could pop out briefly.'

'Is your life really so circumscribed?'

'In a word, Mr Treasure, yes. Mrs Lodey expects value for the money she pays me.' She shrugged. 'And why shouldn't she?'

'And you didn't see Smurt?'

'No. I've talked to him on the phone since. That night he wanted to know what he could do next to win Mrs Lodey over to his scheme.'

'You were sympathetic?'

She nodded in reply. 'I had my reasons. Perhaps rather obvious ones to you.' She paused. 'I have a certain expectation after Mrs Lodey's demise. From her will. That's not wishful thinking. She's told me as much. But it's not likely to materialise if she bankrupts herself on good works, is it?' Miss Modd gave a heavy sigh. 'There, I've told you everything. Are you going to hand me over to the cops? For being out when I said I was in?' She looked Treasure squarely in the eye. 'I didn't kill Angela. I rather liked her. Felt sorry for her, really.'

His hesitation in replying was only momentary. 'I shan't tell anyone else I saw you. Except Molly. It happens I'd told her already. The police interviewed her this morning too.'

'So she may have told them?' The voice was resigned.

'She didn't.'

'You've asked her?'

'Mmm. We've spoken since then on the phone. Your movements that night are really none of our business. And I saw you quite by chance.'

'Thank you, Mr Treasure. I wish I could say I'll do the same for you some time.'

'You never know,' he said lightly, but his expression remained serious. 'I'd still strongly advise you to tell the police yourself. With the reason you've held back till now. It's a perfectly convincing reason. If anyone else saw you and reports it, that could place you in a very invidious position.'

'Since I'm innocent of any crime, not nearly so invidious as Mrs Lodey finding out I deceived her, and deserted my post. You won't tell her either?'

'As you please.' His expression sharpened. 'Tell me, did you see Frakraj when you were in the square alone that night?'

'Didn't see anyone, thank the Lord. Was he supposed to be there?'

'At some time, yes.' He made as though to get up, then asked instead: 'You've made something of a friend of Smurt?'

'Not really. And I don't expect to see him again. Rum chap. Brought out the scarlet woman in me. I flirted with him shamelessly. That scared the pants off him. Not literally, of course. More's the pity, probably.' Her substantial frame shook with genuine mirth. 'Don't believe he'd regarded me as a sex object. I'm not really. Depends on my mood. He got me on a good night. Took me out to a posh dinner. It was all good fun. Except for one bit.' Her face straightened. 'I got cramp in my leg at the end of dinner. Excruciating. He must have thought rigor mortis was setting in on the old girl. It was too humiliating to admit. So I didn't. Don't know what he imagined I was up to.'

'Did you have a more serious purpose in going out with him?'

'Because of his scheme for Saint Martin's? Yes, since it didn't require any of Mrs Lodey's money. We had a mutual cause there, all right. That's why he made such a fuss of me. Anyway, it doesn't matter now. We shan't be hearing anything more about restoration appeal funds. Angela Cudlum's death put paid to that.' She examined her wrist watch. 'I say, isn't it time we went up? Moved Tinder on? Mrs Lodey can't stand him.'

'You're very kind, Mr Treasure.' After shaking hands, Nigel Cudlum responded to the proffered commiseration about his wife. He and Tinder had stood up at Treasure's entry with Miss Modd. 'One has to face realities with vigour,' the cassocked cleric continued. 'Life must go on after adversity. Fortunately I have the challenge of Salchester to occupy me. That's a very great solace. A great looking forward.' An open hand was raised, then closed to smooth the well-trimmed beard in a sagacious sort of gesture.

'That's a stoic attitude,' the banker responded conventionally, but surprised at the evident ebullience in the reply, and the almost debonair resolution of a man so recently bereaved. He accepted that the clergy, having more experience than most others in the handling of grief, would be more adept at publicly coping with their own private sorrows. In that particular, the bonhomie being exhibited by Cudlum was nothing short of exemplary. The thought still occurred, though, that the challenge of Salchester might more logically have been easier to face with a wife than without one.

'Stoicism is an admirable virtue.' This was Lancelot Tinder whom Treasure had just met for the first time. 'I've been trying to impress that upon Mrs Lodey. Just as the Vicar has to soldier on without Angela, so Kengrave Square will soon have to face the future without its little church.'

Mrs Lodey registered tight-lipped contempt over this incautious, tasteless and far from entirely apposite juxtaposing of past and still pending disasters. Then she pronounced: 'The wanton destruction of Saint Martin's will not be tolerated while it can still be resisted, Mr Tinder.'

'I'm afraid I must go,' said Cudlum, hurriedly looking at the time and breaking an awkward silence. 'Another appointment.' He bowed slightly to Mrs Lodey and nodded to the others. 'I can see myself out,' he completed, striding away briskly.

Miss Modd was quickly by the Vicar's side. She left the room with him to apply unnecessary easement to a departure that was already looking more like a successful escape. Her expectant glance at Tinder did not evince the hoped-for sign that he too was ready to go: on the contrary, he had now resumed his seat.

'We came to tell Mrs Lodey that the Parochial Church Council has decided not to press on with any restoration appeal,' said the lawyer to Treasure, with firm finality. 'The remaining churches in the immediate area are so starved of funds, it seems selfish to try raising hundreds of thousands for Saint Martin's.'

'For fear, no doubt, that we should succeed,' put in Mrs Lodey tartly.

Tinder gave an over-patronising smile. 'Ah, always the merry quip. Such acuity, Mrs Lodey.' He turned again to Treasure. 'Seriously, we felt we should formally relieve this dear lady of any continuing sense of obligation.'

'To match every pound raised with two of her own?' asked Treasure, who liked to have things clear.

'Precisely.'

'Isn't that up to Mrs Lodey to decide for herself?'

'But certainly. Except that so far as the parish, and, indeed, the diocesan authorities are concerned, there is no enduring obligation. As her trusted adviser, I'm sure you'll appreciate the distinction, Mr Treasure.'

'You can speak for the diocese?'

'Oh, most certainly. For the Area Bishop himself. Naturally, we want to do everything possible to encourage Mrs Lodey to support the Anglican cause in other needful ways. For instance, Saint Winifred's, Nelson Gardens is woefully short of funds. Of course, it was out of that parish that the greater part of this one was hewn, and to which it will shortly be conjoined again.'

'That remains to be seen,' Mrs Lodey now broke in loudly. 'Saint Winifred's is a church of a quite different tradition to Saint Martin's.'

'Tradition? Tradition?' questioned the lawyer, as though the word was itself unfamiliar to him. 'None of the churches in the local deanery is much more than a century and a quarter old. Tradition would hardly seem— '

'I was referring to the Anglo-Catholic tradition,' the old lady interrupted.

'Which, with respect, isn't much older of course,' Tinder replied.

'The tradition of Catholic worship is as old as Christianity.'

'Ah, the Vicar and I were discussing that point at what must have been the very moment the dastardly crime was taking place.' Tinder shook his head gravely.

'You were together then?' This was Treasure.

'Indeed we were. Or very shortly before. That is if the medical evidence is accurate. And I'm sure it is.' Absently he took a pipe from his pocket, caught Mrs Lodey's deepening frown, and put it back again as he continued: 'I blame myself for not insisting I should go down to the church basement and invite Mrs Cudlum to join us. To talk the matter through as her husband and I had done.'

'You mean you suggested that?'

'Certainly I did, Mr Treasure. Sadly, the Vicar didn't think it necessary. I didn't press the point as I had other business to attend to. I left the Vicarage to call on Peter Windle, only a few steps away.'

'You were in the square at around ten-twenty?'

'For a short time, yes. That would be roughly right. One doesn't consult one's watch at every moment of the day, of course.'

'Have you told the police this?'

'Oh yes. They've interviewed all of us. Isn't that so, Mrs Lodey?'

The old lady raised her eyebrows in a sort of assent.

'Was Windle at home to let you in?' asked the banker casually.

'As it happened, the other chap did that. Denis Hite. They share the house. Peter was on the telephone somewhere. Upstairs I think. He joined us a minute or two later.'

'When you crossed the road from the vicarage, did you see anyone in the square?'

'Frakraj, you mean? No, I didn't. The police asked me that, of course.' Tinder scratched the back of his neck. 'It seemed indelicate to mention when the Vicar was here, but I got the impression they're about to arrest Frakraj.'

'Ridiculous,' Mrs Lodey expostulated.

'Perhaps. But you are altogether too trusting, my dear lady. And tolerant,' Tinder said, again impervious to the wince she gave each time he referred to her as his dear lady. 'He had a motive after all.'

'So did I. So did you,' answered Mrs Lodey hotly.

Tinder straightened in his chair. 'I see no purpose in coining dangerous postulations. Even in jest.'

'I wasn't jesting. We both of us had motives. I had in effect promised Mrs Cudlum two hundred thousand pounds. I might have regretted it, and decided to do her in to . . . to get myself off the hook.' After nodding approval at her own invention she looked defiantly from one listener to the other.

'Except I was with you when the murder took place,' said Treasure.

'You could have been my accomplice.' Mrs Lodey circled the air vaguely with a raised hand that afterwards went to clutch the pearl choker at her neck. 'And don't tell me your wife was here too. All things are possible. The police may have the time of death quite wrong. They're far from infallible.' She flushed a little. 'They made Maud Richly-Hampton's husband a chief constable, I remember, and he was a complete nitwit. Got us lost going to Ascot. Two years running. He'd been in the Blues. Or was it the Royals?' She hesitated, looking about her in mild confusion. For once Mrs Lodey seemed temporarily to have lost the thread.

'Well, the Detective Inspector was more than satisfied about my movements. And where I stand on the future of Saint Martin's,' said Tinder.

'Are you involved professionally?' Treasure enquired, it seemed only out of polite interest.

'It happens my firm handles a good deal of conveyancing work for Aziz Developments in this part of London.'

'Where Peter Windle works?'

'Correct. A very fine company with many interests in the area. They rely a good deal on my advice.'

'And they've been buying up leases and freeholds in Kengrave Square?'

Tinder shrugged. 'I imagine there can be no secret about that.'

'Or of your being on the Pastoral Committee that recommended the closure of Saint Martin's. And on the Planning Committee of the borough council,' Mrs Lodey put in.

'Of course not,' Tinder replied, with volume increasing and coolness evaporating. Even so, he was just able to resist rising too quickly and too angrily to the obvious bait. 'When one is involved in public service, voluntary public service, one has to wear a number of different hats, dear lady. Mr Treasure will understand that. But one is naturally careful to exercise total impartiality if there is any suggestion of a conflict of interest. My legal training has stood me in good stead in that regard.'

'Quite,' said Treasure, thinking the man was too pompous by half, though now seriously ruffled and trying not to show it.

'My husband never cared for me in hats,' Mrs Lodey offered pointedly, with a lift of the head. 'He said they obscured too much of the subject.'

Chapter Thirteen

'The Vicar said to ask, could you call at his house, sir. But only if you had the time, like,' said Henry Pink when Treasure returned to the car.

'Do we have the time?'

'You said to be home by seven-thirty, sir. It's not quite seven yet. Traffic's light. We can be home in ten minutes from here easy, down the back doubles.' He was good at the back doubles.

Pink was not the money-grabbing sort, but both he and his employer were aware that his hourly overtime rate improved substantially after seven o'clock.

'Then ten minutes is what we'll give the Vicar. I seem to devote more time to this church than any of its parishioners. Wonder what he wants?' It was obviously something that couldn't have been broached in front of Mrs Lodey or Tinder.

'Personal matter, he said, sir.' Pink moved the Rolls away from the kerb. 'Did you see the black cloak he was wearing? Cor. And the big-brimmed hat?'

'No, but I think he's quite a trendy dresser, for a man of the cloth.'

'Looked like the bloke in that advert for port wine. Is he the one whose wife got murdered?'

'Yes. He seems to be getting over the shock.'

'Perhaps he puts on a front like? Thing like that stays with you for a long time. Bound to. This is as close as I can get, sir.'

'Good Lord, we there already? I should have walked. Can you stay here?'

'I'll manage, sir.'

Pink had double-parked the car across the end of Kengrave Place, to the right of the vicarage. This alley, some sixty yards long, was a pedestrian way only: there were concrete bollards permanently set here and at the farther Kengrave Road end, to enforce the point on motorists.

Treasure noted that number thirty-eight Kengrave Square was immediately across the end of the alley from the vicarage. He knew that this was where Peter Windle lived. Although hardly elegant, the little terrace houses here were in slightly better condition than their counterparts on the other side of the church, and none had been converted into shops. The shop fronts didn't begin on this side of St Martin's until halfway along Kengrave Place – little shops on the right, with the side windows of the bigger Full Moon Supermarket on the left.

The multi-gabled, Gothic-style vicarage faced the square, although its front door, under a pointed porch, looked onto the alley. The doorway was set back three paces from the street, beyond a paved forecourt. A small red car was parked there at an angle, where it had been driven across the pavement from the square. As Treasure rang the bell he noticed another less elegant doorway a few yards further along. It lay beyond a low boundary wall, and a narrow concrete yard. Absently he surmised that this must be the entrance to the Frakraj flat, above the shop.

'Mr Treasure. It's good of you to spare the time,' Cudlum had thrown open the door with an expansive gesture of welcome. With a bright light haloeing his Messianic features from behind, it was as though he were welcoming a pilgrim on the route to salvation.

'Can't stay long, I'm afraid,' said Treasure, his mind on dinner, not immortality.

'And I promise not to delay you more than is necessary. My study's on the left.' Cudlum motioned the visitor across the hall.

'My chauffeur mentioned it was something personal? If I can . . . oh . . . oh, good evening, Miss Garely?' He was surprised but not at all displeased to find the attractive young gymnast standing in the centre of the study.

Dressed in a form-hugging lemon sweater and straight brown skirt, Kate Garely was brightening the surroundings no end.

The furniture in the room consisted of a steel desk, a filing cabinet, and three upright chairs – cheap, modern, and far from new. Three of the walls were book lined. The grey desk was set under the window and facing it. The desk top held a typewriter, an office tape recorder, a scarred Anglepoise lamp and a scatter of books and papers. The curtains were drawn. They were sombre coloured and very worn – like the square of floor carpet.

'I'd forgotten earlier that you knew each other,' said Cudlum. 'Do sit down, both of you.' As they did so, he turned to Treasure. 'You may not have realised that Kate was my wife's closest friend? A tower of strength to her in every way.' He turned the desk chair to face the others.

'That's an exaggeration,' said Kate modestly, crossing long shapely legs with an audible rub of nylon on nylon. 'Angela doled out more help and strength than she got in return. To everyone. I miss her terribly,' she added, arranging the skirt over her knees before glancing expectantly at Cudlum.

He said: 'Kate has a question, Mr Treasure. It's one I didn't feel entitled to answer on my own. You'll understand why when you hear it. We'd so value your advice. Your being close by tonight was providential.'

'It's about something I saw on Thursday night. After the meeting,' said Kate.

'Some thing or some one?' asked the banker.

'Actually some one.' She gave her head a shake, altering the reflected light on her hair which was drawn back from her forehead to a yellow ribbon at the back. 'You see, after I left Angela— '

'Sorry, what time was that?' Treasure interrupted.

Her face clouded. 'About five to ten. Or a little before.'

'And you left by the steps to the street?'

'No. Through here. Through the vicarage. I'd left my coat in the hall.'

'Did you see each other?'

It was Cudlum who answered. 'No. I wasn't home till a minute or so after ten.'

'I would have stayed with Angela. I wish I had,' said Kate. 'Except she said not to. I can't work a computer, and that was all there was to do. Angela was such an expert— '

'At word processing?'

'Oh, a good deal more than that,' Cudlum broke in. 'She was a computer programmer before we married. Not very senior, of course, but good at it, by all reports. Never managed to teach me even the rudiments, I'm afraid. I'm strictly a two-finger typist with no head for sophisticated machines.' He turned to indicate the typewriter on the desk.

'And the parish desk computer is kept in the church basement?'

'In a small office at the back.' This was the Vicar again. 'At the bottom of the stairs up to the vicarage. It's the part we usually refer to as the vicarage basement.'

'Half-basement really,' said Kate. 'It does have a pokey window onto the little area between here and the super-market.'

'That's right,' Cudlum went on. 'It was more convenient for Angela to work there than up here. Where she could keep an eye on the church basement when in use, and the vicarage, both at the same time. Especially if I was out. The computer's one of the better kind, or so Angela said. It was a gift from a retired parishioner when he moved out to the country apparently.'

'So it was here when you came?' Treasure asked.

'Yes. A definite plus for Saint Martin's, we said at the time. And there weren't many of those, as Kate will agree. In any event, Angela had the computer practically giving organ recitals in no time. Well, after she got the most up-to-date software – programmes, you know? But then, you'll understand it all better than I.'

'Probably not much better, I'm afraid,' said the banker.

'Well, Angela did every kind of job with the machine,' Cudlum enthused. 'The parish magazine. The accounts. Church notices. Tickets for things. Everything. Including illustrated stuff. Saved the parish a packet, I can tell you.'

'Indeed?' Treasure nodded. 'So, please go on with what you were saying, Miss Garely?'

'My friends call me Kate.' She gave him a warm, appealing smile before continuing: 'We'd promised to meet George Rickit and Bernard Nottel for a drink. That's Angela and me. If there was time. In the Bell and Hammer. Angela still had too much to do, but she insisted I went anyway. I didn't stay long in the pub.'

'Did you see anyone else there from the meeting?'

'Yes. The American. Mr Smurt. He was there when I got there. Standing at the bar by himself. He left before we did. That's Bernard Nottel and me. You remember him? He was on the platform for the meeting.'

'And fell off it?'

'Yes.' She smirked. 'Bernard's brighter than he looks, actually. Nice boy with nice manners. He insisted on seeing me home. We left the pub just before ten-thirty. The Bell and Hammer is only a little way along Kengrave Road from the church.'

'Did you have to pass the church to get home,' asked Treasure, and certain that any man who saw the lovely Kate Garely home wouldn't be doing it entirely out of good manners, even a man as young and gauche as Nottel.

'We passed the west side of the church, yes. We were on the other side of the road.' She paused. 'When we were level with Kengrave Place, I saw someone come out of the vicarage.'

'Who was it?'

147

Her gaze dropped. 'I'm nearly certain it was Mr Frakraj.'

'I see. Has he told the police he was here, d'you know?'

It was Cudlum who answered with: 'I'm quite sure he hasn't.'

'And you haven't told them either, Kate?'

'It's something I only remembered today.'

'But the police have interviewed you already?'

'Yes. Mostly about the time Kate and I had supper.'

'We had that together. The three of us,' said Cudlum soberly, shaking his head. 'It was the last time— '

'We had supper early,' Kate interrupted with an understanding glance at the Vicar, 'because Angela had work to do on the word processor before the meeting. I was supervising getting the basement ready generally.'

'And the memory of seeing Frakraj only came back to you after you were interviewed?' said Treasure.

'That's right. It seems so unlikely, I know. But there it is.' She brought her hands together under her chin. 'They asked me to report anything that came to me later.'

'Did Bernard Nottel see Frakraj coming out of the vicarage?'

'I haven't asked him, but I'm certain he couldn't have,' said Kate. 'You see, he was walking on the outside of me on the pavement. Talking to me. He'd have been looking the wrong way to see. It was only a fleeting view in any case.'

Treasure nodded slowly. 'Have either of you any idea why Frakraj was in the vicarage?'

Cudlum said: 'He hadn't specifically been visiting the vicarage. I'd have had to let him in. He must have been using it as a way out from the church. Or the basement.'

'He'd been at the meeting, of course.'

'But he left that with his wife, at the end,' offered Kate. 'They used the main door like everyone else.'

'Except you?'

She shook her head smiling. 'That's right. Silly, I'd forgotten.'

'I see. So he must have gone back to the basement

later. Was he making for the door of his flat when you saw him? It's the one next to here isn't it?'

'That's right, but no. He went the other way. Into the square.'

'Have you any idea why he might have gone back to the basement?'

'Or to the church. The church is more likely. For Frakraj,' Cudlum put in. 'I've no idea why he'd want to go to either. Not at that time of night. All I know is he hadn't been to see me. I was in here at the time he left. With the door closed.'

'Wasn't Lancelot Tinder with you?'

'No. He'd gone by the time Kate's talking about.'

Treasure turned to Kate. 'It couldn't have been Tinder you saw leaving?'

'I'm sure not. You could hardly mistake Mr Tinder for Mr Frakraj, even at that distance.'

'And at night,' said Treasure. There was speculation in the comment, but it failed to provoke a response. 'You said he might have been to the church,' he went on. 'But he couldn't have done that without going through the basement, could he? I assume the church door was locked, while the basement door was still open?'

It was Cudlum who said: 'Frakraj has a key to the south porch door. He's often in the church by himself. For organ practice.'

'I see. That's different, of course. And he'd normally enter and leave that way?'

'Not always. We've never minded his letting himself out through the vicarage. I mean it didn't trouble us. He seldom came in that way of course.'

'Because he'd have to disturb you to open the door?'

'Precisely. But it's obviously quicker for him to use the vicarage. Even one way. Especially in bad weather. It's closer to his flat and the shop than the south porch.'

'You never thought of giving him his own key to the vicarage?'

'Yes. But the insurance company objected to keys being dished out right, left and centre. That's since there was a burglary here. That was before we came. Frakraj could have been a named keyholder, if he'd wanted. But he didn't want, for some reason.'

'So there are some official non-resident keyholders?'

'Yes. The two churchwardens used to have keys. Now it's only the one. Mrs Tinder. The other churchwarden resigned and moved away some months ago. He hasn't been replaced. Not yet.'

Treasure fingered his tie and looked to Kate. 'You haven't told Frakraj you saw him? Asked him what he'd been doing?'

She shook her head. 'I thought of that, but— '

'I advised Kate against it. For the moment,' Cudlum cut in. 'The timing. The fact he hasn't told the police he was in here.' He ended with a shrug and a wide-eyed, pointed stare at the banker.

'I gather someone else has reported seeing him around the same time, but on the other side of the church?'

Cudlum nodded. 'That was Jones. Jones the plumber.'

'You'll remember him from the meeting,' said Kate, then she leaned forward in her chair. 'Do you think I should tell the police? As I said, I'm not absolutely certain it was Mr Frakraj. But nearly.'

'But you couldn't swear to it on oath?'

'I'd rather not have to. That's why Nigel doesn't feel it's fair on Mr Frakraj.'

'Not with so much nebulous evidence against him already,' Cudlum affirmed. 'You see, I find it difficult in my heart to believe he's anything but a good man.'

'On the other hand, you don't want to confront him directly in case— '

'In case he murdered my wife,' Cudlum completed Treasure's sentence. 'And it appears he did have a motive for that.' He gave a sharp sigh. 'If he did do that terrible thing, I certainly don't want him alerted in time to escape retribution.' Now he breathed in and out very quickly. 'Nor do I want him to know Kate is a key witness against him.'

'In case he comes after her?'

'There would be that possibility, yes.'

Treasure sniffed. 'I think you're both being over fair and over cautious. Kate should tell the police straightaway. Let them sort it out with Frakraj. He may admit having been in the church for some quite innocent reason. Also why he hasn't owned up to it already.'

'Because he's been frightened of the implications, you mean?' asked Cudlum.

'Exactly. Anyway, the police are certainly not going to tell him who's supposed to have seen him, so Kate'll be in no danger.'

'But what if they arrest him?' asked Kate.

'If they do that, it'll be on firmer evidence than your saying you think you saw him coming out of the vicarage. It's not strong enough testimony to bring a prosecution. Certainly not on its own.'

'You don't think we'll be guilty of uncharitableness?' This was Cudlum, gravely.

The banker mused for a moment. 'Probably,' he answered eventually, with a shrug.

And Cudlum might conceivably have added inscrutability to the pending charge of uncharitableness, Treasure thought later, on the drive home. Or perhaps that was unfair. The two people he had just left were probably up to nothing more devious than an exercise in passing the buck. And that was something they might not even have admitted to each other.

Even so, it always irritated Treasure when people – especially pious people – went to pains to shift the moral responsibility for doing something distasteful onto some-one else, particularly onto him. And he was quite certain that the interview just ended had not been set up simply so that Kate could elicit his advice.

Both Cudlum and Kate Garely must have known that the police would protect the identity and the safety of an important potential witness. As for the two feeling it would be uncharitable to report Frakraj to the police, morally Treasure felt there was very little difference between that and their deciding to give the same information to himself. This was especially the case since he had a shrewd idea they could have predicted the advice he would give them.

Altogether he had been more than a little disturbed over what had occurred. Now he tried to persuade himself that allowances ought to be made for Cudlum. In the circumstances the man's judgement might well be temporarily impaired. As Henry Pink had wisely observed earlier, the appearance of normality could be a brave front – something that others hadn't appreciated, including Kate. And naturally Kate could have been expected to defer to the cleric's opinion over consulting Treasure in the first place.

Then, just as the car was crossing the King's Road, Treasure was assailed by another more disturbing thought – one that his subconscious had perhaps been conveniently suppressing. Had Cudlum's claimed original charitable attitude to Frakraj been, after all, any different, any less genuine, from his own to Miss Modd over a nearly comparable set of circumstances? Miss Modd whom Treasure had unquestionably seen emerging from Kengrave Square gardens in a covert manner, at that most suspicious of times: Miss Modd who told the police she had been at home at the time of the murder, and only admitted the opposite to Treasure when denial had been pointless: Miss Modd whom he had promised grandly not to expose to the authorities.

So Frakraj was to be reported to the police, while Miss Modd was not – as the result of snap judgements by the same unofficial arbiter, and one who would roundly have defended the impartiality of his judgements in all such matters.

For a moment Treasure came to feel so uncomfortable about the whole thing that he was on the verge of telling Pink to turn the car about then and there, and drive back to Kengrave Square. In the end he didn't do so for several reasons. He had expended too much time on St Martin's already. He was sure Frakraj would be able to provide an innocent explanation for his movements. Deep down he resented being drawn any further into an affair that really was none of his business. And finally, it was nearly time for dinner.

Later he was to regret the decision and to deplore the reasons for it, especially the last and most ignoble one.

Chapter Fourteen

Marvin Smurt's gaze swept down the length of St Paul's Cathedral nave. It reached beyond the great central crossing under Christopher Wren's magnificent dome, moved on past Grinling Gibbons' gloriously carved choir stalls, and came to rest on the high altar canopied by the sumptuous gilt baldachino. But it wasn't the vista that was moving Smurt: he was estimating the value of the inventory.

'Some of us have to make up in practical zeal what we lack in spirituality,' he said, in answer to a question, and speaking in a penetrating stage whisper, while pawing at his moustache. 'Brother Jethro makes allowances for that.'

'Is Brother Jethro very spiritual?' Peter Windle hissed back. He was seated beside Smurt, and, in contrast to the American, his moral sensitivities were being deeply affected by the setting – to a pitch that was already proving uncomfortable.

They were alone in the centre of nearly half an acre of otherwise empty chairs. There were fewer visitors than usual in the cathedral for a Saturday morning – even for a cold Saturday in February. A service had ended ten minutes earlier and there wouldn't be another until evensong. The first convoy of tourist buses had come and gone, in time to catch the Changing of the Guard at Buckingham Palace.

It had been the American's idea to meet here, after his companion had expressed misgiving about their being seen together.

'Brother Jethro is very pleased with the way you've

handled yourself,' said Smurt, without answering the last question.

'Mr Aziz wouldn't be if he knew about our connection.'

'I can't see why not. There's no basic conflict there. Not really.'

'There will be if the Investors for Jesus get Saint Martin's, and Aziz Developments don't. Incidentally, Mr Tinder has a fixation about that too.'

'I keep telling you, it's something we need to take in stages. Anyway, Tinder isn't important. Except maybe to you.'

'That's only for a personal reason.'

'Sure.' The understanding expression was replaced by a quizzical one as the American went on, 'So how exactly is Tinder going to benefit if the sale goes to Aziz?'

'I don't know really.' But the evasiveness was patent.

The noise of Smurt's teeth snapping together was loud enough to set up a small echo from the hallowed walls. 'I believe you do know, Peter. And it's time you levelled with me on that.'

'All right. I think, and that's all, I think Mr Aziz is going to make him a director of Aziz Developments. A non-executive director.'

'But for a fat fee. Well, he can still make it that way in time. And since he'll go on being a lawyer, we'll push some legal business his way. Also in time. The guy could be helpful to us, after all. We have to take the long view. It's all a matter of strategy.' Consciously his gaze now turned to the equestrian statue on the left, halfway down the nave. The effigy on horseback was of the First Duke of Wellington. Smurt didn't know that, but the statue seemed to inspire his next heavily whispered comment. 'Brother Jethro is quite a strategist. Measured against the best of them. Yes-sir.' Then, straightening himself in the chair, he voiced an afterthought with several wags of a pointing finger: 'He has enough spirituality too. Quite enough. You asked about that. Jethro is our power house, no less. And a very refined and cultured human being as well.' Like a guide, he pointed at the figure of Wellington. 'That statue reminds me—'

'Excuse please. John Donne?' enquired the overcoated, earnest Japanese tourist who had quietly sidled up the row. 'John Donne?' he repeated, making a little bow.

'No. Marvin Smurt,' replied the cultured Brother Jethro's disciple with a scowl.

'The John Donne statue is down there on the right,' said Peter.

'On light? Thank you so much.' The grateful enquirer retreated backwards to the aisle to relay the good news to his waiting wife.

Watching the man go, Peter said: 'Well, I suppose if it's only a matter of delaying things a bit. Over Saint Martin's. I mean till Mr Aziz can have the building,' he murmured slowly, as though he was in the process of persuading himself.

'Right. And it's all in his own interests. You still believe these Church Commissioners are more likely to sell to a religious group don't you?'

'On the whole, yes.'

'More so since Mrs Cudlum's death?'

The other nodded. 'But I did say there was no guarantee.'

'Sure, Peter. There's no guarantee of anything. But if you're right, the scenario looks good. We get Saint Martin's because we'll keep it as a place of worship. For a while anyway.'

'How long is a while?'

'A year. Maybe two. Till we can prove it's too small for our needs. Then we offer it to Aziz.'

'At a big profit?'

'For more than we gave for it, sure. Taking into account the improvements we'll make. You remember the parable of the talents, don't you?' Smurt lowered his voice even more and looked about him cautiously, as though that particular piece of scripture might be classified information.

156

'Yes. But it's not specially relevant, is it? Aziz will be knocking down the church.'

Smurt's face registered pain. 'That's an Aziz problem as we see it, Peter. Look, you and I are both accountants. We know the score. You want the Investors' very first deal over here to be profitable, don't you?'

'I suppose so, but— '

'And you also want to be Executive Vice-President of the Community in Britain— '

'I haven't said that,' Peter interrupted in turn.

'No. But you're close to it.' Smurt suddenly dropped a heavy hand on the other's shoulder, making him start. 'You should relax more. You know we were more impressed with you than with anyone else we interviewed a year ago. And you've justified the impression since. I should say more than justified it. So if you're intending to make the lovely Miss Tinder your bride?' He removed the hand.

'There's no question of that. Not yet. Anyway, that's different from changing my job.'

'It has a bearing on changing for more money. Unless you expect your wealthy father to stake you.'

'Not a chance.'

'I didn't think so.'

'And I told you, he's not so wealthy any more. Just celebrated. And a lot less influential. He lost a lot in the big market collapse.'

'And we may be able to help there too.' The American nodded knowingly.

'I don't believe my father would want help with strings attached.'

'No strings. Just an expression of normal goodwill. Mutual goodwill. That's all I meant. And so far as the job goes, from what you said before, it could be a while before Aziz gives you a package as good as ours. But you have to make up your mind. We can't keep a spot like that open indefinitely, you understand? So you going to let me know soon?'

'Yes.'

'And you figure your room mate Denis Hite can take over for us at Aziz Developments if you leave?'

'Possibly. He's not at all religious.'

'Just so long as he can go on feeding us the kind of forward intelligence you gave on Saint Martin's a while back. On CCB and Grenwood, Phipps too.'

'You'd have to speak to him yourself,' the young man answered dully.

'No, I'd rather you did. Don't you see, that's how the Community of Investors operates, Peter? Through co-operation between well-paced executives like you and Denis. In growth companies. Not only well placed either. People with real initiative,' the American was warming to the theme. 'Take the way you used your brains to kill that appeal for Saint Martin's? Boy, you really put that one on the slide. With what you stood up and said that night at the meeting.' His teeth snapped together involuntarily at the satisfying memory. 'I just wish I'd appreciated it more at the time. Might have saved a heap of trouble. Why you—'

Smurt didn't stop speaking, but Peter Windle had stopped listening. 'You didn't have anything to do with Mrs Cudlum's death did you?' he interrupted suddenly.

'You crazy? Of course I didn't,' protested Smurt, louder than he'd intended.

'Nothing at all?'

'Nothing at all. And see here, I don't take kindly to that question. Come to that, I could have asked you the same thing.'

'Except I had nothing to gain by her death.'

'Oh, come on now. We had the same thing at stake. Saint Martin's church. Except you had it on a two-way bet. I don't want to be unkind, Peter, but the way things stand, you're winning if either Aziz or the Investors get the place. And that Mrs Cudlum appeal could have stopped either one of us getting it.'

'The appeal will fail because Mrs Cudlum died. Not because of what I said at the meeting.'

'Well there you seriously underestimate yourself,' the American supplied, in the cause of strategic magnanimity.

But it was the last unctuous comment that made the young accountant finally decide that he'd had enough of Smurt – and divided loyalties. 'I don't underestimate myself,' he said, trying to keep his voice modulated. 'But I think the Investors have overestimated my talent, and a few other things about me that aren't so noble. Thanks for everything, but I don't want that job.'

'Hey, don't rush things like that. I didn't say I needed to know today.'

'I haven't rushed. I've been building up to that decision for a week. I don't think I'm right for your organisation. I've had too many doubts since that Thursday night. About what happend then. I can't explain how I feel. And I can't stop you getting Saint Martin's. That's if its offered. But I hope it isn't. I'm only sorry I tipped you off about it in the first place. And about the CCB and Grenwood, Phipps involvements.' He stood up, flushed but adamant.

'Peter, I— ' Smurt was searching around for his coat, and then for his scarf which had fallen under the seat. In any case, his rejoinder was unexpectedly submerged by a triumphal opening bar from the great organ of St Paul's. It was the start of a spirited rendering of a J. S. Bach toccata and fugue, intended by the assistant organist to uplift hearts on this dull Saturday morning.

The music allowed the already coated Peter to exit smartly with an excuse for not hearing any more of Smurt's parting argument. He left the confused but powerful American upending a metal seat leg in a final effort to retrieve his scarf – which resulted in the whole connected row of chairs tipping over with an unholy clatter, audible even above the organ notes.

A frowning verger was hurrying to the scene as Peter

strode away appearing both relieved and buoyant – even though that last impression was deceptive.

Smurt had been too close to the mark with one of his comments for Peter Windle to be complacent.

'In the end, I felt very badly about letting Cudlum and Kate Garely turn Frakraj in to the police,' said Treasure, who was driving.

'So now they've let him go you can feel good again,' Molly replied, making a face at herself in the mirror on the inner side of the car sun-visor. 'They *have* let him go, you said?' She smoothed away some superfluous eye make-up with a finger tip. 'That's better,' she said. 'We left in such a hurry. It was that phone call.' She rehoused the visor, and settled back in the front passenger seat.

The two were heading out of London for Saturday lunch at the home of friends near Windsor Great Park. 'They kept him all night for questioning at the police station,' said Treasure, swinging the Rolls left from Warwick Road into West Cromwell Road. 'He doesn't think they believed his story. Or so Mrs Lodey just told me on the phone.'

'But they still let him go?'

'Presumably because what evidence they've got wasn't strong enough to justify an arrest.'

'The evidence being that Kate saw him coming out of the vicarage at half past ten?'

'Which he denies. And that's only partly it. He doesn't know it was Kate who informed on him, by the way. But he says whoever it was must have mistaken the door to his flat for the door to the vicarage. It's what I suggested might have happened. The doors are very close.'

'And he was coming out of his flat at half past ten?'

'He says not, although it could have looked that way. He says he went back to the door at about that time, after he'd been for a walk a bit earlier. I suppose that fits better with Jones saying he saw him near the church porch around ten-fifteen.'

'But Jones hasn't said he saw Mr Frakraj go down to the basement?'

'I don't think so. Anyway, instead of going into his flat when he got back, Frakraj insists he turned around again and went back to the square, meaning to call on Mrs Lodey.'

'At that time of night?'

'It does seem unlikely. But Mrs Lodey is known locally to be a late bird.'

'But why hadn't he called when he was out the first time?'

'He says it took him the best part of a quarter of an hour to work up the courage.'

'Ah, that I can understand. I assume he wanted to talk to her about Saint Martin's? About the appeal. Perhaps to cancel his donation?'

'That could be right, though he hasn't said so specifically. But it seems he decided he really had left it too late when he saw us leaving in the car.'

'Although we didn't see him. Poor Mr Frakraj. And all because Kate thinks she saw him doing something he says he wasn't. Would it have helped if he'd seen Miss Modd or this Mr Tinder? They seem to have been playing hide-and-seek in the square at about the right time.'

Treasure thought for a second. 'I saw Miss Modd coming back through the gardens at twenty past ten. That was about the time Tinder says he crossed from the vicarage to Peter Windle's house. Yes, Frakraj could have caught sight of either or both of them, I suppose, but it seems he didn't.'

'So it's all to do with Jones seeing him on one side of the church, with Kate saying he came out of the vicarage a quarter of an hour later?' Molly questioned slowly.

'Yes. With the Cudlum murder taking place in between. And put that way, I must say it sounds bad. In a sense, he's lucky not to have been arrested.'

'Not lucky if he's innocent,' Molly retorted hotly. 'And he's poured all this out to Mrs Lodey this morning?'

'To Miss Modd, actually. In the shop. When she went in to buy tea,' Treasure frowned. 'It's all very muddled though.'

'But quite obviously genuine. I mean it's too muddled to be planned. Could you turn up the heating a bit, darling? I hope I'm going to be warm enough in this dress,' Molly added.

'Looks warm enough to me, and it's a bit late to do anything about it now.' He was just accelerating the car up the approach to the M4 motorway.

'I wish Beatrice and Reggie weren't such martyrs to the flesh. I really believe they think keeping their house warm is wicked in some way.' Molly was musing about the couple they were about to visit. 'Wicked or unnatural. Like . . . like watching television in the morning. Or having sex in the afternoon.'

'If your first contention about them is right, it might be too cold for the other two. In the winter anyway. I always think living in a Grace-and-Favour house like theirs, courtesy of the Queen, could make a lot of things sort of lese-majesty.' He paused. 'Going to bed with Beatrice at any time of the day would certainly be one of them.'

'That's not fair,' Molly protested. 'She can't help being regal. She was brought up to it. Her father was a colonial governor. One of the last. Anyway, I always thought you rather fancied Beatrice.'

'Too many teeth.'

'Oh no,' Molly answered with total assurance. 'Toothiness is a very attractive feature in a woman. Not so much in a man, perhaps.' She pondered for a moment. 'Spotty's a bit toothy.'

'Who?'

'Spotty Nottel. The Saint Martin's treasurer. But I've rather warmed to him.'

'I believe he's probably making a play for Kate Garely.'

'Well he's wasting his time if he is,' Molly observed flatly. 'Apart from anything else, she's too old for him.'

'Not by much surely?'

'I meant mentally. Did I tell you he rang me again yesterday afternoon?'

'I don't think so. Nor at the other times. Assuming there were some,' came the purposely light rejoinder. 'If he's making a play for you too, don't you think you're a bit— '

'Too old for him?' Molly interrupted. 'Oh, very droll. I was sure I'd told you he'd been on to me about the Saint Martin's appeal? I said if it goes ahead, I'm still good for the money I've promised. He and old Mr Rickit also want me to be chairwoman of the appeal committee. I said I would if they really want me. D'you mind?'

'Of course they'll want you. They'd be daft not to. And I think I can survive the resulting protests.'

'Who from?'

'The army of Grenwood, Phipps customers who want the church knocked down.'

'Didn't you say Jumbo Crib-Cranton was one of them?'

'Yes.'

'Well, dear Jumbo adores me.'

'Unfortunately he's not the only one. I don't mean the only one who adores you. I mean not the only customer wanting the church knocked down. Anyway, I'm sure it's all academic. The Diocese isn't going to rescind that redundancy notice, so your appeal won't get off the ground. I told you, Tinder is roundly against it.'

'Tinder sounds quite odious.'

'Mysterious too. Did I tell you he had a lovebite on his neck? Last night at Mrs Lodey's? A fairly fresh lovebite at that.'

'Well it wouldn't have been made by Mrs Lodey.' Molly chuckled. 'You sure? Lovebites in the afternoon? But he sounds altogether too— '

'I tell you, it couldn't have been anything else.'

'His wife's the churchwarden.' Molly paused while they both considered the implications of that fact in relation to lovebites. 'Perhaps their house is over heated,' said Molly finally.

Treasure grunted his amusement. 'Anyway, Tinder, odious or otherwise, is very influential. And I suspect he speaks for the majority over the appeal. Including those who volunteered contributions merely as a timely gesture of support for Mrs Cudlum.'

'That doesn't include Mrs Lodey or me?'

'No. And Mrs Lodey definitely doesn't care for Tinder.'

'That's what I mean. Fancy opposing a generous old lady like that? Well, whether the appeal goes ahead or not, I'm perfectly willing to help get the paperwork sorted out. Spotty Nottel finds that a great, unexpected bonus. Mrs Cudlum did all that kind of thing. Now everything's in the computer, but there's no one who knows how to retrieve it. That's according to Spotty.'

'And what a mine of information he is. Was he surprised about your being a computer queen?'

'Fairly. Most people are. They never understand why one has learnt to operate a word processor. Especially this one,' she concluded huffily.

'Wait till the play you've written is televised, then they'll understand,' said Treasure.

'If it ever is televised.' Her third attempt at a TV script had been accepted by the BBC, but it had yet to be produced. 'I've established that the computer software Angela Cudlum was using is the same as mine,' Molly went on. 'Except they say she'd customised it.' She saw him wince. 'All right, horrid ugly word, but it's very apposite.'

'And means she'd enhanced what was there already with systems of her own invention? Doesn't that faze you a bit? In case it's very sophisticated? She was a professional computer programmer, after all. Her husband told me.'

Molly shrugged. 'Doesn't bother me. It's just a challenge. I have to retrieve her drafts that's all. Shouldn't take long to find. Oh, and several lists of names she'd been putting together.'

'Well, I hope you won't be wasting your time.'

'I have a bit of spare time next week. To devote to good works. Before we go into rehearsals on Thursday.' She fell silent for a minute, studying the snow-covered fields on either side of the motorway. The road was dry but there had been more snow since the thaw of the previous week. Then suddenly she asked: 'If Tinder was at large in Kengrave Square at the time of the murder, why haven't the police hauled him in for interrogation as they did Mr Frakraj?'

'He's been questioned, like everyone else.'

'But everyone else wasn't lurking about at the critical time. It hasn't been a case of colour prejudice operating against Mr Frakraj, has it?'

'I'm sure not,' said Treasure, who had a wholesome regard for the impartiality of the Metropolitan Police.

'Nor class prejudice favouring Tinder? Lovebites and all, he sounds very Establishment.'

'That wouldn't affect police attitudes these days.'

'But you believe Tinder's going to benefit in some way if the church is sold to Aziz Developments?'

Treasure nodded grudging assent. 'It's only a gut feeling. And a highly libellous charge to make against a borough councillor. So don't— '

'Tell anyone else you said it. OK. But if he's a crook, I hope he gets found out. And if he's a murderer— '

'No doubt he'll get caught,' he interrupted with a frown. 'To tell you the truth, I'm much more concerned about the innocence or otherwise of Miss Modd.'

'Who you could have turned in? As Kate did Mr Frakraj, you mean?' Molly shook her head. 'Not the same thing at all. There were too many people involved over Mr Frakraj. Better it all came out in the open. But you were free to make up your mind alone over Miss Modd. And you decided she couldn't do murder in any circumstances. I agree too. Entirely.'

'I thought I'd decided that, which is why I promised I

wouldn't mention seeing her to the police. Now I wonder whether she wasn't being a bit too glib to be credible when I talked to her yesterday.' He paused. 'Remember, she was a nurse? Mrs Lodey happened to mention that again last evening.'

'You're thinking of the accurate bash with the slate? Plenty of people in West London have a working knowledge of anatomy and physiology.'

'But only Miss Modd stands to inherit the whole of Mrs Lodey's estate.'

Molly looked surprised. 'Everything?'

'Mmm. Not just a substantial legacy. The lot. Mrs Lodey mentioned that too. It's been bothering me ever since.'

Chapter Fifteen

Kate Garely, in a red track suit, was jogging effortlessly, but not yet at the even pace employed for the serious part of her weekend work-outs. There were obstructions, too many pedestrians and too much traffic, as she weaved a way from her flat in Thornhill Road down the most unsalubrious section of Kengrave Road, past the tube station, and over several more crossing streets. She was making for the Old Brompton Road.

'Late today, miss. I'm just packin' up,' called the burly, emphysemic newsvendor on one of the corners. He was seated, flat-capped and muffled beside his stacks of news-papers and a rack of mostly soft-porn magazines. He gave Kate a look that combined admiration and carnal desire in just respectable disproportion.

'I lay in this morning, Joe. Naughty,' she sang back cheer-fully: she was usually out before breakfast on Saturdays.

'I wondered about you.' He wondered about her quite a lot, and wished he'd been lying in with her this morning and all. He'd have 'naughtied' her all right, he calculated lewdly, wheezing over the cigarette clamped between his lips.

It was three-thirty. There were plenty of shoppers about, and many more street idlers – mostly teenage lads hanging around the garish cafés and shops, eating, or drinking from cans. The shop fronts were litter strewn, and the wide pavements beyond cluttered with shiny printed adver-tising messages, in metal frames or hand-lettered on tent-boards, offering 'Instant Passport Photos' and 'Double

Cheeseburgers 90p' and 'A week in Majorca £78'.

Predictably, only the cheeseburger sign was generating evident consumer response.

The pants of Kate's elasticated suit offered tight, well-shaped buttocks, thighs and calves working in what the newsvendor and an increasing platoon of young male observers found to be richly stimulating unison.

Kate was conscious of her good looks and body, and if she was openly contemptuous of the wolf-whistlers and the catcallers, she was not unflattered by their attentions. Even so, she was out for exercise, not to arouse sexual interest. This was something it became fairly necessary to insist on later – in view of what happened.

'West London and Westminster Cemetery. Erected 1839' read the legend. It was hewn in the frieze above the opening of the mock triumphal-arch-cum-columned-gatehouse of the massive burial ground. Kate used the pedestrian crossing in Old Brompton Road opposite the gates and paced on through the arch, lengthening and settling her stride.

At first she joined the wide, straight beech-lined avenue that runs down the centre of the flat, enclosed, twenty-five acres. This main carriageway finishes more than a quarter mile distant in front of the domed chapel known as the Octagon. The building, and the crescents of roofed colonnades that preface it, were only dimly discernible now, in the gathering dusk, beyond the files of leafless trees.

Soon Kate swung left off the main avenue onto a narrower path that ran close to the walled and railed boundary. Following this, she would be giving the chapel complex a wide berth, going around behind it, close to the other main cemetery entrance – to the south on the Fulham Road – and circling up the other side to where she had started. She intended to cover this one mile circuit, or a similar distance on different paths, four times before the place closed at four.

Some might not consider a cemetery the most congenial place to take exercise, especially in the late afternoon in mid-winter. But the grid of well-kept, dissecting paths in this one offered an interesting variety of routes, with the metalled, cambered surfaces drying out quickly after wet weather. Altogether there was the atmosphere less of a burial ground than of a city park – and an agreeably deserted one. The place's original function had in any case long since ceased to apply in any very active way. All available plots had been sold before the end of the previous century. Now only occasional interments took place where there was still space in family vaults or graves for the few still entitled to use them.

There was a curious serenity about the tombs arranged in ranks, but with a pleasing if predictable absence of uniformity in size and shape. The memorials were in the main substantial and Victorian – romantically embellished, statued, scrolled, and inscribed with extravagant eulogy that time and the elements had, in most cases, done little to obliterate.

Those whose remains rested in 'The Brompton', as it's known, had paid (or, more accurately, pre-paid) for enduring memorials, with the homilies and notations for posterity deep-etched or heavily glazed, or both.

On the first circuit, Kate encountered only five people – two male joggers chatting breathlessly to each other, a bow-legged elderly woman walking a bow-legged elderly dog, and an entwined pair of lovers progressing at an appropriately funereal pace but otherwise too involved with life to be conscious of the evidence of death on every side.

This was the normal kind of attendance roll for the time of year. It was close to freezing, and there was still some snow capping most of the memorials, though the paths were entirely clear. Kate was attacking the last with great energy.

She enjoyed the privacy here, but never felt isolated. There was always the buzz of the traffic from outside, but there was more than that today. Chelsea Football

Club was playing at home, at the Stamford Bridge Stadium that backed onto the far, south-west side of the cemetery. Frequently the air was rent by the roar of the fifty-thousand-strong crowd there. Kate was a Chelsea supporter who seldom attended matches. Even so, she knew that this match should have been over by now, and must have run into extra time.

Kate didn't see Sundar Frakraj on her first circuit of the cemetery. But that wasn't surprising.

Frakraj was well hidden, not far from the central avenue, and a hundred yards in on the right from the Old Brompton entrance. Even if Kate had jogged by on that route, which she hadn't done yet, he'd have been screened from her sight.

The Sri Lankan was seated, not very comfortably, inside the two-columned portico of a dressed-stone edifice of classical shape and inspiration – one of the most grandiose family vaults in the cemetery. It was a miniature model of a Greek temple, the size of a biggish garden summer house, though built of more enduring materials. The proportions were not quite right of course: Frakraj had noted as much – specifically that the pedimented portico covered a third of the building's length: otherwise it would have been difficult for someone of his size to sit beneath it. The ledge on which he was perched was barely a foot wide, but the semi-enclosed area was quite large enough for what was intended to follow.

No one at all had passed since Frakraj's arrival, although his required view was not onto the central avenue but onto the parallel one next to it. The vault occupied the space of two normal burial plots which is why it straddled the width between the two paths.

The door to the vault was at the opposite end to where Frakraj was sitting, which in time past must have allowed for more direct, uncluttered access for coffins than would have been possible if the door had been at the porticoed end. It also provided direct access to the central carriageway and thus, probably, a marked degree of extra status.

The grave on the right was adorned with a life-sized angel holding a lettered scroll. While he had been waiting, Frakraj had occupied his mind by several times deciphering the wording on the scroll in the failing light: there was really nothing else to do.

'In fond memory of Richard Winthrop Smith,' read the angel's scroll. 'Born Paris March 18th 1852, fell asleep at Folkestone June 2nd 1896. The Lord gave and the Lord hath taken away.' Which Frakraj mused meant it was all God's fault not the railway company's.

He looked at the time again. He had arrived earlier than was necessary. That had been on purpose. It shouldn't be long now.

'You're not relaxed? I can always tell.' She leaned over and ran a hand down his naked body, at first letting the fingertips just touch him, then the nails, as the hand went lower over his stomach, then lower still.

He wriggled to indicate pleasure, but the movement wasn't convincing. 'Of course I'm relaxed. Well, perhaps not completely.' He brushed both sides of his moustache and stretched his neck, in two characteristic gestures.

Lancelot Tinder – senior partner of Tinder & Company, Solicitors, borough councillor, elected member of the General Church Synod, co-opted member of the Diocesan Pastoral Committee, and sidesman elect of St Winifred's, Nelson Gardens – never wholly enjoyed the post-coital phase in his lovemaking with Mrs Deirdre Peckworthy.

It wasn't that he was tired of her. It had been the same from the beginning. Come to that, it had been the same with his wife, also from the beginning. Except with Enid he'd never exactly been ecstatic about the *pre*-coital phase either – or the bit in the middle come to that, at least not nearly so much as with Deirdre. Naturally he blamed Enid for that. She had never been adventurous in bed. She wasn't creative about it. He always considered the shortcoming was a consequence of Enid's too middle-class upbringing.

Tinder's upbringing had been very similar to Enid's.

Of the three of them, it was only Deirdre Peckworthy who actually provided what Tinder regarded as a creative approach to the matter of satisfying his sexual needs.

Mrs Peckworthy was senior secretary at Tinder & Company, and, in a manner of speaking, legal mistress to the senior partner. She was thirty-nine years of age, originally from Lancashire, happily divorced and continuing in that state from choice. Her figure was statuesque, her flesh firm, considering her age, and her proportions only a fraction less than Amazonian. She had jet-black hair, a passionate temperament, and the good sense not to be over demanding of Lancelot Tinder who was a fine provider, and, for that matter, a good employer. He was often an exhaustible lover, but you couldn't expect everything.

'Heavy problems pressing on your mind, love, I expect,' she said, shifting her body on top of his once more.

'Yes.' He stared woodenly at her large breasts resting on his chest, not far from his chin. They were supported from beneath, but not covered by the leather brassière and halter, the only part of the slave-girl outfit that hadn't been discarded during their recent quite lively congress. He liked Mrs Peckworthy to dress up for the occasion.

'Anything I can do, love?' Gently she massaged his temple, her elbows still mostly supporting her weight.

'Nothing really.'

Nothing, he thought bitterly, nothing that would make up a shortfall of half a million pounds – the sum he'd appropriated from one of his client's bank accounts.

Tinder was especially glum and introspective because this was the moment when guilt always assailed him most. It was not the guilt of his just having been unfaithful to his wife again. That would only have applied if he'd had no more besetting things on his conscience, and perhaps not even then.

The embezzled half million was something he'd been living with for so long now he had almost become inured to it. Until recently he had been sure the money would be replaced before the loss could possibly have been discovered. He had confidently expected to cover it out of his profits in the futures market.

It was in the futures market that Tinder had lost the money in the first place. But like many unadmitting gamblers, he had an enduring belief in the ultimate soundness of his own investment judgement.

He had started 'borrowing' after the stock market tumble a few years earlier. At first it had been a hundred thousand to tide him over. Then the total had crept up inexorably as a succession of speculative investments had gone sour. Trying to recoup after each failure had simply landed him with greater losses that he couldn't cover from his own resources.

He had only 'borrowed' from the one client – the only one where he could be certain he could get away with it. The client was a widow, now living in Amersham. She was not enormously wealthy, but comfortably off. She left all her financial affairs in Tinder's hands on the instruction of her late husband. There were no complicating trusts, and no children either.

On her death, the widow's estate was to be divided between a handful of deserving small charities whose trustees knew of the expectation, and the approximate size of the capital sums. But the promised donor's demise had seemed to be years away: she was a mere and vigorous sixty-two.

Tinder had long since stopped providing annual accounts for the lady to examine. This was on her own instructions. She claimed that she couldn't understand them so there was no point. Simply she expected him to keep her capital intact – another of her husband's strictures – and to make sure it generated enough income for her to live on. Tinder had provided the income all right, except that latterly most of it had come from capital not earnings. Now there was scarcely any capital left. But there had been no one to find out.

It was the classic swindling of an unquestioning client by an unscrupulous professional adviser – not an uncommon case, excepting that in this one, three weeks before, the vigorous widow had been found to be suffering from a wasting disease. Her doctors were not hopeful of arresting the condition, and the lady had very sensibly informed her solicitor. If she expired the officers of those worthy charities would soon be looking for their legacies, or demanding to know why the widow's promises were not being kept.

'It's nearly four. I'll have to be going soon,' said Tinder, stirring from his unnerving contemplation.

'Already? Have a cup of tea first.' Mrs Peckworthy kissed him on the lips. She was disappointed but resigned. 'Stay there. We'll have it in bed. Won't be a minute. I've made some of your favourite cakes.'

She gathered up the slave-girl discards, the minuscule leather skirt, the leg-strappings and the thonged whip, before padding out with them.

He watched her go. She was wearing well – better than Enid, but then Enid was a lot older. He wished he could dare share his present besetting problem with Deirdre: she had a very understanding nature.

The bedroom was cosy, like the rest of the attic flat on the third floor of the Tinder offices, in a narrow terrace house off the borough High Street. It was a small flat, but adequate for one – convenient too, for a conscientious secretary with a boss who often required her to work over the lunch hour, in the evenings and at weekends. As everyone accepted, including his wife, Lancelot Tinder's voluntary work for church, charity, and community allowed him very little leisure time. The light in his second-floor office could be seen burning at all kinds of irregular hours. It was even burning there now.

'Any more news on Mrs Cudlum?' asked Deirdre

Peckworthy, reappearing a few minutes later dressed in a shorty silk gown. Her hair was pinned up in oriental fashion now, and held in place by prominent silvered combs. The gown was decorated with dragon designs and had a gold sash. This was her geisha-girl outfit, including the fan hanging from her right wrist. She placed the laden tea tray she was carrying on a bedside table before joining Tinder on the bed again.

'I haven't heard anything on the murder,' he said, looking at her with growing approval.

'Case of the police being baffled. Too many like that these days. Enid was saying the same on the phone in the week.' She poured tea into both cups.

Comments involving Tinder's wife were commonplace between these two at the office, and had come not to seem incongruous or in dubious taste in Mrs Peckworthy's bed.

'There's no reason to suppose the police have given up. Not yet.'

'Except if they don't get a lead on that kind of crime pronto, it never seems to get solved. Sit up and have your tea. Shall I put one of these fairy-cakes on a plate?'

'Thanks.' He had decorously covered his lower half with the quilt.

'It was a mugger right enough. Don't you think? Though why he went for poor Mrs Cudlum we'll never know,' she went on, without waiting for an answer to the question. 'Didn't look like she had two ha'pennies to rub together, I remember. That once when she came to the office.' Mrs Peckworthy paused to sip her tea. 'Still, lucky you were accounted for. At the time she was done in. Awkward otherwise.'

He looked at her sharply over his cup. 'I was with her husband.'

'I know, love. That's what I mean. Marvellous they get the time of death so accurate these days. It said in the paper.' She swallowed more of the tea. 'Mmm, that's good. Doesn't half make you thirsty.' She rubbed a bare leg against his.

'Which paper?'

'The local. You saw it. I showed you.' She watched him nod. 'And the police are asking about everyone connected with the church being closed. Mavis Chorlton, the Bishop's secretary, she told me that.'

'When?'

'Yesterday afternoon. I rang her to find out if they'd heard anything from the Church Commissioners. You said to keep asking.'

'That's right,' he answered absently. His thoughts switched to the money he'd been promised if the whole St Martin's deal went through. It was substantial – not enough to make up all that he'd embezzled, but enough if matched with a story he could concoct about the widow sustaining investment losses.

Having the church formally considered for redundancy had been his idea in the first place – not that anyone would ever be able to prove it. It was also he who had put Akro Aziz onto developing the area, of buying leases as they came up, of putting in the kind of advance plans that the borough council could accept. As vice-chairman of the borough planning committee he had been able to steer through the decisions in the matter himself – but again in the most covert way, over a long period.

He had never attempted anything so ambitious before. Nor had he ever needed the reward for such initiative so urgently.

It was only a matter of time now. He was reasonably certain of that. But time had become the essence. It depended on how long the widow lingered. If she expired before the St Martin's deal was completed, he was going to ask Akro Aziz to advance him his share. Their agreement had been on payment after results: it was why the pay-off was to be so large. A directorship was part of it, but that was only decoration: not that he belittled anything that went to

176

improve his status. Aziz Developments were going up in the world: he'd be happy to ascend with them. Meantime, he hoped Mr Aziz would not insist on clawing something back in exchange for early payment.

At least there was hope again now, when a week or so before he'd been in despair. The tea and cakes were helping to revive his spirits. Involuntarily, his legs moved closer to Mrs Peckworthy's.

Angela Cudlum's appeal could easily have wrecked everything, of course. Altogether her ending had to be regarded as a timely if unpleasant necessity. The more he steeled himself to that opinion the more he was coming to accept it.

'So who's going to be Ensign Pinkerton, 'cos his Mimi's waiting? Not sailing for home yet, are we? Not after all?' Mrs Peckworthy had disposed of the tea things and the quilt. She was kneeling astride Lancelot Tinder and starting to do exciting things with her geisha fan.

Chapter Sixteen

Bert and Lily Dawes had been married thirty-eight years and lived in Kennington, near the Oval. They were in their Austin Mini, on the way west to Hammersmith for tea and an evening of whist with Lily's sister Beryl and her husband. Bert had chosen Old Brompton Road to avoid the football traffic in Fulham – at least, that had been the idea.

'It's like rush hour here,' said Mrs Dawes, looking up from her knitting. 'Can't we go that other way?'

The single-line traffic was at a standstill as far as you could see in both directions.

'Can't turn round here. Wouldn't have been any different. Even in Warwick Road. The match must have run late. We'll have to lump it now.' Bert Dawes was a fatalist by nature.

'Nobody walking, of course.' It was true that the pavements were almost empty. Old Brompton Road wasn't a shopping street. Mrs Dawes pursed her lips. 'Never had no car when you went to football.'

'Lot of things we didn't have then. After the war,' said Bert. 'Good little bus this, though. Seen us through a lot of traffic jams.' He smoothed the steering wheel which had a leather cover. Their oldest grandson had given them the cover for Christmas. Bert wasn't sure he liked the feel of it, but it would have meant disappointing the youngster not to use it – for a bit anyway. They'd bought the Mini second-hand nearly six years ago. But it was immaculate. Bert polished it every Sunday, including in the winter.

Their council flat, in a high-rise block, had garages for the tenants at the back.

Mrs Dawes frowned again at the traffic. 'Should have started earlier. I did say.'

'I remember,' Bert agreed absently. He usually did. It made for a quieter life. He was a telephone-repair engineer who got enough aggravation from customers in his job. He went on watching the impatient-looking Jaguar driver immediately behind them.

'You can go, you know, Bert?' his wife admonished.

He had still been looking in the rear-view mirror. The line of cars in front of him, held up by a just-out-of-sight traffic-light, had vanished. No sooner had Mrs Dawes issued the irritated alert than the Jaguar driver swung out, and, with a burst of acceleration, bore past the Mini that Bert was wrestling into motion.

'Stop, Bert! Oh my lor!'

Instead of speeding ahead, the Jaguar was now screeching to a halt, spinning around in front of them: the Mini was aimed to crash into its shining nearside.

The cause of the calamity was only too clear to the occupants of both cars in the split second they had to digest it.

A young woman, hair over her face, and clad in a torn red track suit, had burst blindly through the cemetery gates, crossed the narrow slip road, and staggered on over the pavement and into the main road. She had been heading into the path of the Jaguar, but, just in time, drew back again, as though sensing the big car before seeing it. Then she wavered, hand to head, before collapsing in a heap, half on the pavement, half in the gutter.

'Oh my lor!' said Lily Dawes again. The Mini had also finished up half on the pavement, at right angles to the road. Bert had dexterously steered it there miraculously undamaged – in spite of the leather wheel-grip – but after a very nasty jolt.

'You all right Lil?' he asked.

'No thanks to him in front. Ought to be locked up.'

'Don't think he could have—'

'That girl needs help,' Mrs Dawes interrupted, thrusting aside her knitting and undoing her seat belt. 'Wasn't our fault, remember,' she cautioned sternly.

The Dawes's reached Kate Garely first. Her body was shaking with violent convulsions. 'Keep him away . . . he tried to kill me,' she sobbed.

'Calm down, lovey. You're safe now. Quite safe. We'll look after you. Nothing to worry about no more,' Mrs Dawes crooned to the victim she was soon cradling in her arms. 'Was it rape, dear?' she added in a softer voice, and frowning at her husband who looked embarrassed.

'Ask if she's hurt then.' Bert was kneeling too, but drew back slightly. He had been close enough for Kate to have caught his question without the need of an intermediary, but he didn't want her to think he might hear her answer about being raped.

Kate stopped sobbing. The shaking too was less violent and only intermittent. Involuntarily, she tried to pull together the parts of the track suit. The top and pants had been ripped on one side. Still bewildered, she blinked up at her comforter. 'In . . . in the cemetery,' she breathed, fingering her neck. 'A man attacked me. He'll be in there still.' Then she caught her breath at the sight of the blood on her hand.

'I've sent for the police.' The Jaguar driver had joined them and was standing over the three. 'D'you need an ambulance? I can phone again from my car. If you want to go to hospital. Or I can take you. Better be on the safe side.' He had an educated voice. The authority in it seemed to rally Kate. He had asked her the question direct. If you looked well enough to decide whether you needed an ambulance, she thought, you couldn't be at death's door.

A group of onlookers was gathering.

'I'll be all right. I think. I was frightened.' Kate gave a

deep swallow, looking at the Jaguar driver. 'It wasn't your fault. I'm sorry I ran out like that. If the police could—' She took a painful breath. 'In the cemetery.'

'No one's come out since you did,' said the Jaguar driver. His car was jammed against the kerb, just beyond Kate and immediately opposite the cemetery gate.

'He'll have gone by now. There's another gate,' volunteered a male bystander at the front. 'Other end. On Fulham Road.'

'Gate's closed down there. Always is on Saturdays. Before the game's over,' said another man, much younger, in a leather jacket.

'So let's go after the bastard,' shouted his companion.

The two youths broke away and turned for the gate.

'He could be over the wall anywhere,' the first speaker called after them.

'Here's the police,' shouted someone else. 'Better wait lads.'

Mrs Dawes continued to hold Kate in her arms. 'No need to talk now, lovey. Save your energy. Best to go to hospital. For a proper check. But I'd wait for the ambulance.' She glanced down meaningfully at the torn pants, then flashed an ominous look at her husband before adding, 'It's only a little scratch on your neck. Nothing to worry about there.' She dabbed again at the cut with her handkerchief, being careful not to let the blood touch her own skin. As she told Bert later, you never knew what you could pick up these days where sex fiends were involved.

While the uniformed policemen were still getting out of the patrol car, and the two youths were standing irresolute in the slip road, three men appeared through the cemetery gateway. They were walking in line abreast. Two of them were also in police uniform. It wasn't at first clear whether these two were holding the man sandwiched between them, or whether they were simply supporting him.

The man in the middle was Sundar Frakraj.

* * *

'Except Frakraj didn't know it was Kate Garely who'd informed on him before, sir,' said Detective Inspector Daynon.

'About seeing him coming out of the vicarage. Around the time of the murder?' Detective Superintendent Welling hadn't needed to check this with the report on his desk, nor any other point so far. He had a nearly photographic memory for detail. His meeting with Roger Daynon had been going on for over half an hour already. He had read the seventy-page document as soon as it had been delivered to his Putney home. That had been late the night before.

Welling, in his fifties, was a stout, jolly man with kind eyes and not much hair. He was head of the CID for this Sub Division of the Metropolitan Police. Serious crime on his patch was up this year already by seven per cent, and unsolved serious crime by twenty-three per cent. It was detail like that he'd much rather be able to forget. He was determined to improve on the second statistic in every way open to him. This was the reason he was in the station so early on a Sunday morning. He had wanted first hand elucidation from Daynon, the Senior Investigating Officer on the Cudlum case, of the surprising but unactionable conclusion at the end of the report.

It would not normally have been up to Welling to do the appraising at this stage on a case, except the Detective Chief Inspector to whom Daynon should have been reporting had been laid up with a stomach ulcer for three weeks. And it hadn't helped that they were one DCI below strength already.

'You can never be certain if a suspect's worked out who's done the fingering, Roger.' The shirt-sleeved Welling leaned forward as he spoke, scratching his back vigorously. 'Worked out, or found out.' He respected Daynon but found him a cold fish, lacking in human understanding.

'Frakraj couldn't have found out from us, sir. I put special wraps on.' Daynon sat even more upright in front of Welling's desk, aware that the point was wide open to challenge.

'He doesn't need to have been told, of course. What if he saw her on the night? The same time as she saw him?'

'I think he'd have admitted being in the vicarage, if he really had been there. When we told him he'd been seen. There was someone else with Miss Garely who knew Frakraj.'

'Nottel. The parish treasurer.' Welling wiggled his shoulders before leaning back in his chair.

'That's right, sir. Frakraj could have seen him as well as the girl. He might have thought they'd both said he came out of the vicarage. If it had been true, I still think he'd have come clean about it.'

'Instead of trying to brazen it out. Saying he was coming out of his own doorway, after going up to it, and coming away again.' Welling shook his head. 'I found that part hard to swallow at first.'

'He's very credible under questioning.'

'Credible or plausible?' The Superintendent smiled. 'You think he was set up in the cemetery all right?'

'With the phone call. Yes, I do.'

'That was at one o'clock yesterday? An hour after you'd had him in for questioning and let him go. And the caller could have been either sex, he said. Disguised voice, anyway. And he was told . . . ' This time Welling flipped back a few pages of the report before continuing. 'Told to be at a special tomb in the cemetery, directions supplied, at three forty-five. Someone was to meet him there and give him the names of the people who'd been smashing the windows of his store in Cordley.'

'It was his wife who eventually persuaded him to ring us, sir. She was suspicious. So two observers were sent.'

'Uniformed constables. Sounds a bit daft for an undercover job.'

'It was very short notice by the time he rang. They were

on the spot. Or close by. Part of the detail covering the match at Stamford Bridge. There's plenty of cover where they were hiding.'

'And nothing happened. Except the girl got assaulted close by. From behind. In the dusk. Assailant unidentified.'

'That's right, sir. Frakraj would have been accused of that if we'd found him inside. If he hadn't had witnesses. Police witnesses. She could have been murdered.'

'Why wasn't she, I wonder?' Welling pulled his chair closer to the desk. 'Don't misunderstand. I'm glad she wasn't murdered. Bloody glad. What with two coppers observing tombstones a hundred yards from the scene. But what was the purpose? Rape couldn't have been made to stick. If Mrs Cudlum's killer was setting up Frakraj for the first crime, why didn't he do a proper job on Miss Garely? You'd only just let Frakraj go for lack of conclusive evidence. Doing in the best Crown witness against him so far could have solved that problem for us all right.'

'The murderer might have meant to kill her, but she was too fast for him, sir. It's why she didn't get a proper view of him.'

'And our two intrepid officers never chased him?'

'They didn't know exactly what had happened till later. Miss Garely never screamed. Just ran. The constables were alerted to the situation by radio, after a nine-nine-nine call. They went to where they'd been told they'd find Miss Garely.'

'Taking Frakraj with them?'

'Yes. They went straight back to the cemetery afterwards. And they were heavily reinforced within minutes.'

'But whoever it was got clean away. I suppose it couldn't have been Frakraj all the time?'

'Not possible, sir.'

'Or pretty impossible. The girl doesn't like him. That's clear enough.' Welling fished out a fat stubby pipe from the top drawer of his desk. 'So it's lucky Frakraj has a cautious wife who makes him report things.'

'Epsom police say he's regularly reported all threats and harassments to the business down there.'

'All? What sort of threats and harassments?'

'Anonymous racist letters. Bomb threats on the phone. Stones through the windows. Dog shit through the letter box.'

'Epsom.' Welling pronouned the word as if he'd been hurt. 'And half the parish of Saint Martin's knew Miss Garely would be jogging in that cemetery at half past three. Because she told them.'

'Afraid so. It was one of the things she talked about in the church basement earlier. She was there between ten and twelve yesterday morning.'

'Doing what? Doesn't say here.' He tapped the report but didn't re-open it. He was resting his tobacco pouch on the cover while he filled the pipe.

'Sorry. She was in charge of receiving and sorting old clothes. Stuff being brought in for a jumble sale they're holding on Wednesday night. It was one of the things Mrs Cudlum had organised. Miss Garely had taken it over. There were a lot of people in and out.'

'Including Frakraj?'

'No. His wife was there very briefly. Although she said she didn't hear Miss Garely talk about her plans. Plenty of others say Miss Garely was joking about sorting jumble being easier than her regular five-mile jog. And that she'd re-scheduled that for three-thirty.'

'Why that specific?'

'She was running an extra aerobics class in the basement at two-thirty. That was after she'd made lunch for the Vicar.'

'Such energy. And devotion.' Welling had struck a match and was waving away the smoke as he applied the flame to his pipe.

'The whole cemetery episode could have been coincidence, of course,' said Daynon. 'Pretty lady in sexy track suit, jogging in a deserted place.'

'You mean a sore temptation to a few thousand frustrated yobbos just let out from a football match next door? Mmm. Without the Frakraj involvement I'd agree. As it is, he must have been set up by someone.' Welling sucked hard on the pipe. 'That coloured lad whose knife was found in Mrs Cudlum's hand— '

'Barclay. He's in the clear over her murder. So far as we can tell. He and his mate Hawker were in a snack bar, with four others. From the end of the church meeting till just before they found the body. The snack-bar owner's confirmed it. Barclay had dropped the knife in the basement during the meeting. Mrs Cudlum must have picked it up. She'd have known it was his. It's his carving knife. Wood carving. That's his hobby.'

'She'd have known that? Conscientious vicar's wife, of course. Familiar with the habits and pastimes of the parishioners. Except she wasn't regarded locally as the perfect soul mate for the Reverend Cudlum in his new job.' The speaker looked up sharply. 'And does he really get fifty thousand pounds from that private insurance policy he had on her?'

'Yes. And that's on top of what he could have got from the church insurance. If her death had been an accident.'

'Fifty thousand. It's a tidy sum. Thought it might have been a misprint in the report. Must have cost a lot in premiums. Had the policy long had he?'

'Four years. It's a life policy only, but convertible to endowment any time during the first ten years. Unless that happens the premium's quite low. A hundred and fifty a year.'

Welling gave a grunt. 'Four years. Too long for her death to look like a connected event, especially if he's canny. Or perhaps he just needed time to drum up the courage to do the deed.'

'He *is* a clergyman.'

'So was Rasputin.' Welling laid a flat hand on the

report. 'According to what's here, he had the motive, he could have had the opportunity, and, like anyone else, he could have come upon the weapon.'

'Except— '

'Except we'd have a hard time proving it. And there are several more runners with better form, even though you're not backing any of them. Councillor Tinder seemed a likely lad to me. Still does.'

'We're waiting for more about him from the Fraud Squad, sir.'

'But you've got enough already to prove motive. That bank manager must be wetting himself. How is it he didn't know he had a solicitor customer who's been liquidating client securities and putting the proceeds into his private account? I mean, it wasn't hundreds of pounds. It was hundreds of thousands. Doesn't the bloody manager know his bank's liable over that kind of caper?'

'He doesn't know anything yet, sir. Not for sure. The Fraud Squad's confiscated all the data, and he's been told by his head office to keep his mouth shut.'

'I see. Anyway, if Tinder's done murder, the embezzlement will be a sideshow. Also the yet-to-be-proved gentleman's agreement with Mr Akro Aziz. Incidentally, judging from that interview report, Mr Aziz will be throwing Tinder to the lions in the very next round.'

'We think so, sir.'

'Which should put Tinder's seat on the borough council on the line. Not to mention his church appointments. None of that's our affair of course. Nor his relationship with his secretary.' Welling did some tutting. 'Bloke like him ought to realise what being caught up in a murder hunt's going to uncover.'

'I think he's pretty desperate. The Fraud Squad reckons his pay-off from Aziz over the Saint Martin's property deal is his only hope. And has been for some time. It could be very big money.'

'Big enough to motivate murder? The opportunity was

there, too. Between the time he left the Vicar and the time he got to Windle's house across the road.'

'It wasn't long, sir.'

'He didn't need long.'

'We're still working on him.'

'Do that, Roger. It could pay off yet. This Peter Windle isn't important? His dad is. You know that? Not that it matters.'

Daynon nodded. 'Windle was on the phone to America when he said he was. From ten-o-five to ten twenty-two. British Telecom have confirmed somebody was, from that number.'

'And the only other person in the house was the joint tenant Hite. He answered the door to Tinder.' Welling hesitated as if he was about to pursue the point, then he made a dismissive gesture with his pipe before commenting: 'And Marvin Smurt isn't as important to this Jesus group as he makes out?'

'He's very much on trial as the Investors for Jesus international director. He brags a lot. Gave us a lot of confidences which he hoped we'd respect.'

'That's like asking a tart to hold your wallet.' Welling chuckled. 'I noticed he said the Investors would soon be one of Grenwood, Phipps' biggest clients.'

'And that Windle is about to join his staff. Both statements have proved to be inaccurate, sir.'

'And the Saint Martin's deal is the first he's ever done for the Investors outside the USA?'

'That's right. So it was important.'

'But not important enough, according to your reckoning.' Welling held up his hand to stem whatever the Detective Inspector was about to answer. 'You're probably right. But he was the last person known to have seen Mrs Cudlum alive.'

'He left her at ten, observed by Jones from his window. Smurt was in the Bell and Hammer two minutes later, where he stayed— '

'Until he left at ten-sixteen, in front of Miss Garely and Nottel. They saw him turn down into Kengrave Square where he said he'd parked his hired car. Seems to go out of his way to be noticed, would you say?' The Detective Superintendent saw Daynon look at the time. 'All right, Roger,' he continued quickly, without waiting for a reply. 'Smurt doesn't interest you. Nor do any of these others really. Not nearly so much as your prime suspect, anyway. Even though they all have more going for them in terms of straight motive and opportunity.'

'I'm sorry, sir. I accept I'm leaving more to prove, but I've got a gut feeling— '

'And don't you ever be ashamed of that, laddie,' Welling interrupted, thrusting himself forward and spreading both arms across the desk. 'It's the most exciting thing you've said this morning. Gut feeling's a valuable commodity in any copper's make-up. So cultivate it. But let's talk about facts as well.' He leaned back again. 'I agree you could argue the lady had a motive of sorts.'

Chapter Seventeen

'Miss Modd was very lively and amusing at breakfast.' Treasure examined the tip of the billiard cue, rubbed more chalk on it, blew at the result, then perched himself on a bookcase in the small office he had just entered.

'Wasn't she trying too hard? Nervous tension, I thought. Because we both know her guilty secret, perhaps.' Molly pushed the spectacles down her distinctly patrician nose, looking over them and away from the screen of the desk computer in front of her. 'And is this supposed to be the coffee break? Because if it is, there's no coffee.'

'No. Purely a social call. Just wondered how you were getting on.' He brandished the cue. 'I'd forgotten what a dab hand I am at snooker.'

'Even without an opponent, you mean?' said Molly, drily.

'An opponent wouldn't have got a look in with the breaks I've just had out there.' He paused, eyebrows lifting. 'Well, hardly a look in.' He gazed about the room without enthusiasm. 'D'you know, I can't get over what happened to Kate Garely yesterday.'

'Or Mr Frakraj.'

'Both.'

'But the lovely Kate appeals more to your protective instinct,' Molly offered with a dazzling smile. 'I'm just glad Mr Frakraj didn't get arrested again.'

'They didn't arrest him before. Just had him in for questioning.'

'But someone must be gunning for the poor man.'

'Looks very like it. Kate was composed enough in

church. I mean, one wouldn't have known anything had happened to her. And she didn't mention it when we were coming out.' It was Mrs Lodey who had given them the story over breakfast.

'In many ways, Kate's a very private person,' said Molly slowly. 'Miss Modd said she only found out about her new job because of a friend teaching at the same school.'

'Curious the police didn't find another soul in that cemetery.'

'It's a big place.'

'But very difficult to get out of once the gates are closed. Or so Miss Modd told me. She was once locked in there. After spending too long in the lavatory. She really is a caution.' Treasure chuckled. 'She says the walls and railings would be very difficult to climb.'

'For her, perhaps. Not for a mad rapist.'

'Kate wasn't raped. Or much harmed.'

Molly leaned back in her chair. 'Would you say the whole thing could have been a put-up job?'

'No. She's hardly a frustrated virgin. Is that what you mean?'

Molly shrugged. 'Don't know what I mean really. Shouldn't have said it. Crossing with your protective instinct.'

'I see,' he replied amiably, without really seeing at all. 'So, are you nearly through, or should I set up another snooker frame? You said half an hour.'

'I know, and it's after ten already. I'd no idea it'd take so long.'

The Treasures had joined Mrs Lodey and her companion at the early Sunday service in St Martin's, breakfasting afterwards at Kengrave House, all by prior arrangement. The two had later returned to the church, and gone down to the basement. The Vicar had provided a key to the office there then excused himself to brush up the text of his sermon for the eleven o'clock service. Molly had wanted to spend a little time familiarising herself with the

191

word processor before coming to work on it in earnest the next day.

The office was cramped, but also pleasantly warm. There was carpet on the floor, and an oversized radiator on the outside wall. Apart from the bookcase, most of the available space was taken up by the single pedestal desk, at which Molly was seated, and a low, steel filing cabinet. The computer printer was on the cabinet. The small window was barred; its top reached to ceiling height. What view and illumination the window might have provided were largely blocked by a very large dustbin outside. A single electric bulb in a ceiling socket was providing the working light.

'Give me another five minutes could you, darling?' Molly asked. 'If I haven't cracked Mrs Cudlum's codes by then, I'll leave it, and ring Miss Gaunt for help in the morning.'

It was Treasure's secretary who had taught Molly how to use a word processor.

'Mrs Cudlum used codes? Sounds like espionage,' commented Treasure.

'As a member of the ignorant management class, I suppose you can't be expected to understand the jargon of the working girl in the electronic age. Or her problems.' Molly made a face at him, re-adjusted her spectacles, and applied herself to the screen again, making tentative taps at the keyboard below it.

'Try me.' He squeezed behind her chair.

'All right.' She leaned back with a sigh, and evidently quite disposed to share the reason for her frustration.

Her husband studied the close-set prose illuminated on the screen. 'Is that a page for the parish magazine?'

'Right first time. The magazine must be what the computer's been mostly used for. This model's a more expensive version of the one I have, but it's not terribly different. The word-processing software is exactly the same as mine.'

'So, where's the problem?'

'The problem is, Mrs Cudlum was a computer buff. She improved the software, by building in programme changes of her own. Refinements.'

'That's what professional computer programmers must be doing all the time. In this case, to what purpose?'

'To cut corners, I should think. To speed things up. It's basically a simple sort of word-processing system, and a bit slow. That's what our Miss Gaunt says. Compared, for instance, to the IBM machines in your office.'

'I should hope so, too, at the price.' He pouted before continuing thoughtfully. 'So what you have here is a standard sort of computer. But fitted with an improved brain, known in the trade as software?'

'Which comes on these little disks.' She fingered one of the slim, square plastic plaques lying on the desk. 'The trouble is, Mrs Cudlum didn't leave any guide to the changes she made.'

'Didn't need to, because nobody else used the machine?'

'Probably. But I can't even get access to her files. Well, only the directory of some files I don't need.'

'You've tried that filing cabinet?'

Molly emitted the understanding noise a parent makes when a promising infant bravely attempts some task beyond its mental or physical capacity. 'The directories I need stay inside a word processor, darling. God, you really are ignorant,' she said.

'Not at all. I'm too expensive to be bothered with trivia, that's all,' he answered with mock pomposity.

'Well, for future information, when you need computer directories, you bring them up on the screen. By pressing keys. Not by opening drawers and fiddling with papers.' Her brow knitted. 'Except the only directory I've retrieved so far only covers stuff for the parish magazine. Want to see it?' She pressed two keys on the computer keyboard. The image on the screen changed: instead of a page of consecutive prose, it now displayed columns of data.

Treasure squinted at the screen over Molly's shoulder.

'Times, dates, reference numbers, and short descriptions of individual items,' he said. 'That's clear enough. Even to an ignoramus. Do you always note the time and date of everything?'

'No. You don't have to. Not for the directory. They're put on automatically. There's a clock and calendar built in. Set for years ahead. For ever possibly. The one on my machine even adjusts itself for British Summer Time. And Leap Year. The time and date's always right. I expect this one's the same.'

'I see. And all those references relate to items for the magazine?'

'Mmm. To articles, lists of church services, the roster of altar-flower ladies, prayers for Lent, and so on.'

'No use to you?'

'None. Except perhaps the prayers if I can't get an answer any other way,' she said ruefully. 'I want the directory of the appeal stuff. For instance, there's an appeals address list Mrs Cudlum was working on. She'd also drafted different sorts of appeal letters aimed at different kinds of donors. She was a very literate person, by the way. I've been reading some of her own articles for the magazine. Like the one on the screen just now. They're good. Out of the rut. I'll bet the appeal letters are good, too. If I can find them.'

'Aren't there printed copies of them already? Something of the kind was being passed around at the meeting.'

'Those were copies of the draft petition. She wrote that just in time for the meeting. It's first rate. I've got a copy. But there's no directory reference printed on it. Probably because she forgot to put it on in the hurry.'

'You said that was automatic?'

'Not on the printed document, it isn't. Only on the directory in the machine.'

'How complicated. And the other things you mentioned? The letters?'

'It doesn't seem she ever printed out any of them. Probably she didn't bother while things were in draft form.'

194

'But you can retype the petition on the word processor, and print all the copies you need of that?'

Molly nodded. 'But it's not the same with the address list or the letters. And Mrs Cudlum had worked so hard on them, according to Spotty Nottel. For instance, to find possible donors, she was researching from the Saint Martin's marriage register. Taking the names of everybody married in the church over the last forty years, then trying to trace them on to their present addresses. She was doing the same with the baptismal register.'

'Very smart.' Treasure continued to study the screen. 'So how d'you get to directories on your word processor at home?'

'Oh, that's easy. As soon as the software's loaded from the disk, the Master Menu comes on the screen.'

'The what?'

'The Master Menu.' She grinned. 'That's what it's called in computer-speak. And that's its title on the screen. It's a numbered list of main subjects, set out just like a menu.' She paused. 'Let's see, at home, my subjects are TV Play, Diary and Correspondence. That covers all my big involvements. And Miscellaneous covers the rest.'

'And each subject has its own directory?'

'Yes. And when I start work, I just choose the subject I want from the Master Menu.'

'And that doesn't happen with this machine?'

'No, it doesn't. There's no menu. It goes straight to magazine work every time. If I key in the directory, it's always the directory of magazine items.'

'You think because Mrs Cudlum was mostly working on the magazine, she cut out this Master Menu sequence altogether?'

'Made a way of going round it, yes. To save time. But that menu has to be in there somewhere. She certainly covered plenty of other things besides the magazine.'

'That's right. Her husband told me as much.' Treasure's brow creased. 'In fact, it's pretty difficult to understand why this parish needs a magazine at all. I mean, hardly anyone seems to go to church.'

'Ah, but hundreds who don't go to church will subscribe for a magazine. It's a conscience salver,' Molly provided knowledgeably. 'Same in most parishes these days. By coughing up two pounds a year for a monthly magazine, people feel they've done their bit to support the church.'

'Even if that's their only contact with the church?'

'Better than no contact at all, most vicars would say. It means those parishioners aren't totally beyond their reach. Those magazine subscriptions can add up to quite a lot, too. Then there's income from advertising. From local shops.' She nodded her head. 'It's all worthwhile. So I can understand why Mrs Cudlum worked so hard on the magazine. What I can't credit is the absence of directory entries on this machine covering other work. The appeal, for instance.'

Treasure pondered for a moment. 'Just now you pressed two keys to get the parish magazine directory,' he said. 'Which keys were they?'

'This one marked Control, then the D key. D for directory. It's quite logical.' She had pointed to both keys with a well-manicured forefinger.

'Have you tried the M key? M for menu?'

Molly shook her head. 'It wouldn't work. You shouldn't have to strike a letter key for the Master Menu. It comes on automatically. Either in the sequence after the software's loaded, or at any other time by pressing the Escape key.'

'There's an escape key? We're back to espionage.' He squared his shoulders and folded his arms. 'All right, just to indulge me, will you use the Escape Key to go back to where the Master Menu ought to be?'

'Won't do any good,' she said. But she did it anyway, with a resigned expression.

'OK.' Without studying what was now on the screen,

Treasure leaned over and pressed the Control key, then the M key.

Instantly the screen was displaying the heading MASTER MENU in capital letters above a list of subjects.

The word APPEAL was third on the list and numbered accordingly.

A digital clock was pulsing out the seconds in a corner of the screen, just under a display of the date in figures.

'My hero,' cried Molly, unstinted praise being preferable to excuses and mortification. In any case, humility was not her style.

'It was nothing, really,' Treasure replied lightly, reaching again for the billiard cue. 'The obvious is often a less attractive challenge than the obscure.'

'Yes, darling. But don't get too heady about it,' she took one of his hands and squeezed it. 'Oh, and that's the clock and the calendar I mentioned. They only ever appear on screen with the Master Menu.'

A minute later Molly had already had a selection of appeal items displayed in turn. 'So it's all here,' she said with enthusiasm. 'The letters. The address list. Everything. Marvellous. We can go home now.' But she was still giving a last look at the appeals directory which she had just brought back to the screen.

Treasure was looking at it too. 'Have you noticed that Mrs Cudlum didn't really get to work on the appeal till the week before she died?' he asked.

'Except for the address list,' Molly agreed, glancing at the times and dates before each item. 'That was started four weeks ago. Probably the address list was her special job when Mrs Tinder, the churchwarden, was still queen bee of the appeal. Which she was until her disapproving husband warned her off. D'you remember Mrs Lodey told us?'

'I think so,' he answered absently, his mind preoccupied with something else. 'About this clock, it works off a long-life battery, not the mains, of course.'

'Why?'

'Because when we came in, you had to switch the power on from the wall plug. There was no mains power to the computer till then, but the clock was showing the right time when it came on with the Master Menu.'

'And the right date,' said Molly. 'D'you know, I've never realised that before. It's the same with my machine at home, of course. If we're away, I always turn off the power at the wall.'

'But the clock goes on working. Nothing magical about that. Except, presumably, one day you'll have to change the battery. D'you know where it is?'

'No, but I'd get a man in for that. I know an awfully good one.' She chuckled, turning her head to look at him. 'That was meant to be a joke.'

'This isn't, though.' He pointed to an item in the directory. 'This is the reference to the petition Mrs Cudlum composed on the night of her death?'

'Yes. It says "Petition" in the last column.'

'Look at the time and date she started it.'

'At nineteen-o-two on the sixteenth. That's significant?'

'It's more than that. It's critical.'

'You mean— ' but she stopped what she was saying and looked towards the open doorway. 'Why, good morning Mr Frakraj. Are you all right?'

'Mrs Treasure. Mr Treasure. Good morning.' A harassed-looking Frakraj came further into the room, closing the door behind him. 'I've been in a quite terrible dilemma. Quite terrible. There was no one I could speak to. Not even Mia, my wife. Then I heard you were here. What a blessing. What a godsend.'

Chapter Eighteen

It was a quarter of an hour later when Treasure tapped on the open door of the vicarage kitchen, upstairs, at the end of the corridor. 'Hello, Kate. I was told I might find you here.'

Kate Garely had been standing with her back to the door at the table in the centre of the room. There was an apron tied at her slim waist, over an off-white knitted dress with a V-neck and flared skirt. Her hands were kneading something in a basin.

'Hello, Mark. Come in. I'm cooking between church services. Well, the better the day the better the deed.' She looked about with a smile. One flour-covered index finger delicately tidied away a long, wayward lock of hair from where it had fallen, beguilingly, across her face. 'How was breakfast at Kengrave House?'

'Almost baronial. Eggs, bacon and sausages under silver salvers.' After closing the door behind him, the banker moved to stand at the end of the table. 'What are you making?'

'Pie crusts. Steak-and-kidney pie's one of my specialities. Nigel has to be fed. He's one of those men who scarcely knows how to boil an egg. The ladies of the parish have to keep him supplied with easy eats.'

'Ladies in the plural, or is it mainly you?'

Her gaze went back to the basin in front of her. 'Mainly me, I suppose. I owe it to Angela, you see?' she added quickly, and just a shade defensively. 'She was my friend after all. But there are others who help. Nigel's very popular, you know? It's a pity the church is so unattractive.

That's the reason it's empty. Not the Vicar.' She presented the last contention in a way that nearly made conviction a substitute for credibility.

'Perhaps he'll be more appreciated in Salchester. I hear you're on your way there too?'

Her gaze came up. 'Who told you that?'

'Is it supposed to be a secret?'

'It's just that I'm not sure I'm going any more. The job there. It was something arranged before Angela died. She wanted me around.'

'To give her support in a new rôle she found daunting?'

'Something like that.'

'Except she might not have been going herself. From what she said at the end of that meeting.'

Kate shook her head. 'Staying on here would only have been a temporary thing. Even if she'd done it.' She lifted the pastry mix from the basin and dropped it onto a board ready for rolling.

'That was a curious experience you had in the cemetery last evening.' He moved to lean against the sink, which put him directly opposite Kate, across the table.

She turned her head so that he could see the sticking-plaster on the side of her neck. 'Curious wasn't the word.'

'I thought it appropriate. What made you do it?' The question was offered in a deceptively casual tone.

'Do what?' she asked, rolling the pastry with a touch more vigour than before.

'Tear your clothes. Scratch your neck. Run screaming into the street. All before staging a very uncharacteristic collapse in the gutter.'

'Are you serious?' She had stopped all movement and was looking him straight in the eyes, in total astonishment.

'Perfectly serious. You were seen.'

'By whom?'

'By Sundar Frakraj.'

'That little swine?' she replied, dismissively. 'Sorry, I

200

thought you were being serious. You know I can't help feeling bitter. To think he's still free.' She let out a sharp, angry sigh. 'It *was* him you know?'

'Who attacked you? But that can't be true. He was under police observation the whole time.'

'All right. It was he who arranged it. With one of his awful relatives probably. There are dozens of them.'

'Why would he have done that?'

'To scare me off from testifying against him. Or to shut me up altogether. To murder me. As he did Angela. And all for greed.'

'Those are very dangerous accusations. I don't believe he had anything to do with the murder. And I don't believe you do either. And you certainly know he had nothing to do with what happened in the cemetery.'

'So why was he there?'

'Because he was sent by whoever arranged what followed. That was you, wasn't it? I've told you, Frakraj saw you.'

'How could he have seen— ' she began vehemently, then stopped in mid-sentence.

'How could he have seen you, when you were fifty yards from where he was supposed to be waiting? And well screened? Well, despite the directions, it seems he got the tomb wrong. Or the vault. Or whatever it was. And the path. He got that wrong as well. Though he found one of each that seemed to him to fit the description perfectly. You were barely ten yards from him, and in full view, when you cut yourself. And your clothes. With nail scissors, I gather. Which you then threw into the bushes. They'll still be there, I expect,' he ended coolly.

'Somebody tried to grab me, I tell you. From behind. With a knife.' She was flushed and very angry, but she had failed to disguise a brief, startled reaction at the mention of the scissors. 'Oh, this is ridiculous. If Frakraj saw me, why didn't those police watching him see me too?' she challenged, doing her best to recover her composure.

'It was your good luck that they were watching the west side of the tomb, from a fair distance away. They were expecting someone to approach it from their side. You passed to the east of it, on the main pathway. They couldn't see you. But Frakraj could. He'd got bored by the one outlook. It seems he was looking right at you round the side of the place.'

'So why didn't he tell the police this?' she questioned hotly.

'Strangely enough, to protect you. Your reputation. He's a very tolerant and compassionate man. And he genuinely cares for you. One wonders why. Though I did think from our conversation here on Friday you were quite concerned not to get him into trouble.'

'That was Nigel, not me. Well, perhaps I didn't want to be the one who got Frakraj accused of murder. Not then. It was a matter of simple charity. Misplaced charity, of course,' she ended, tight-lipped.

'Anyway, he hasn't told anyone yet about seeing you in the cemetery. Except Molly and me.' Then he hesitated before adding. 'As a matter of fact, he thinks you may be ill.'

'Me ill? I suppose he means insane? Bloody nerve, coming from him,' she answered vehemently. 'He's the mad one. I mean, it's no thanks to him I'm not in a hospital. Or a morgue.'

Treasure remained expressionless. 'When you were making lunch here yesterday, did you ring Frakraj from that phone?' He nodded towards the wall-receiver near the door. 'At exactly one o'clock?'

'Why should I have rung him? I've been trying to avoid him. He told you this too, I suppose? You ought to know, it's hopeless believing anything he says? He's a liar. Can't you see that?'

'Frakraj didn't tell me. But I believe the police will prove someone rang his flat from this number. Could it have been Nigel Cudlum? From his study?'

She stiffened for a moment. Then her gaze dropped before she offered carefully. 'Nigel could have rung, I suppose. Yes, he might well have. He often has to speak to Frakraj.' She swallowed. 'About the music for the services.'

'This call wasn't about music. It was about going to the cemetery at three forty-five. Unwittingly to be set up on a charge of . . . ' He shrugged. 'Assault? Rape? Attempted murder? You tell me. I don't know.'

'You're making this up. You can't prove Nigel or I made any call.'

'Quite right. I can't. Not yet at least. I've still to prove the call came from this house. But I'm sure it did. And it won't be difficult for British Telecom to check it out. They already know the time, and the number where the call was received. They'll shortly have the number from where it originated.'

'Except that won't prove what Frakraj says. About his being told to go to the cemetery. You've thought of that, I hope?'

'Naturally. Anyway, it's not important now? Not any more.'

'Well I'm glad to hear you think so,' she replied with some relief. 'So can we please stop playing silly games? I tell you, I couldn't care less about Frakraj's lies.'

'I'm afraid it's one of your own . . . inaccuracies I'm concerned about.'

'I've told you, I didn't call— '

'Concerning the time you and the Cudlums ate on the night Mrs Cudlum died,' he interrupted. 'You told the police you all started a sandwich supper at ten past seven. I believe Nigel confirmed the time later.'

'That was when we ate, yes. Or thereabouts.'

'No, not thereabouts. I think the police told you how important it was to have that time right?'

'All right. If it's so crucial. It was ten past seven, as exactly as I could remember. So what?'

'So you must have been mistaken. You and Nigel.' The young woman looked up at the emphasised last remark, and as Treasure went on. 'How long did you take over those sandwiches?'

'Look, I don't have to tell—' She stopped in angry mid-sentence, then began again in a more controlled tone. 'A few minutes. Five perhaps. Not more. We were all in a hurry.' She picked up the rolling-pin again and applied it to the pastry mix with unnecessary vigour.

'In a hurry because Nigel was late for his lecture, and you and Mrs Cudlum had a lot to do in the basement? Before the meeting?'

'That's right.' As if to demonstrate that she was finding the questioning a lot less involving than her cookery, she went over to the refrigerator, took out two small, oval pie dishes already filled with ingredients, then returned to the table with them.

'So on your reckoning, Mrs Cudlum started work on the word processor in the office a little after seven-fifteen?'

'I suppose so,' she answered, now in a preoccupied tone. She was laying a pastry covering over the top of one of the pies.

'Except she actually began the work at two minutes after seven.' He waited before adding. 'And, I should warn you, that is eminently provable.'

'Indeed?' Kate looked up, meeting his gaze with a wide-eyed and almost patronising smile. 'Then I must have made a mistake, mustn't I?' she said, before returning to her task.

'It seems you both did. You and Nigel Cudlum. Over something that has a profound bearing on who could and who couldn't have murdered his wife.'

She stopped moving the fork she was using to decorate a pie crust border. 'I don't see how that can be?'

'I think you do. You're aware that the time of death was fixed through your vouching for the time you all ate. That was in spite of the body temperature putting the time of death as fifteen minutes earlier. But that wasn't thought as reliable as the deductions the police could make from your evidence. Possibly you know that?'

She looked up. 'No. Why should I?'

'I was guessing. I understood you graduated in physical education and in dietetics.'

'Which doesn't cover anything as morbid as the state of dead bodies.'

'Sorry. It would cover anatomy though?'

'PE does, yes. Except I don't see— '

'The new evidence will put the time of the murder at five past ten,' he broke in. 'Or two minutes either side. You realise that rules out Frakraj as the murderer? Also a number of other people.'

'Lucky for them. Except nothing will persuade me it rules out Frakraj.'

'It not only rules out him and others. It brings one or two in.'

There was silence between them for several seconds. Then Kate said: 'I don't believe I was wrong about the time we ate. Angela could easily have been working in the basement before that. I mean, who's proving she was down there at seven and stayed there? She could have come back up to eat. I really don't remember that clearly.'

'I've told you, the evidence of her being there at seven is incontrovertible. As for her staying there, whether she did or not, she'd eaten before she went down in the first place. Her husband told me she was here in the kitchen ironing for some time before you came by and made the sandwiches for everyone. That after you'd all eaten, Mrs Cudlum went downstairs. You followed her a minute or so later, after you and he had another cup of coffee.'

'When did he tell you this?'

'A few minutes ago,' he answered quietly. 'Was it in that minute you were alone that he persuaded you to say you'd eaten later? That you agreed, without understanding at the time you'd be giving him an alibi for murder?'

'Oh my God.' The fork she was still holding fell from her hand, clattering to the floor. 'Is that what Nigel said? Tell me, is that what he's said?' Both her hands were clasping the edge of the table. Her body had begun to tremble. She looked up at him, pleading for an answer to the repeated question, but getting none. 'Well, it's not true,' she insisted. 'You've got to understand, it's not true. Nigel wasn't involved. It wasn't him who persuaded me to say when we ate. It was the other way round. He didn't remember what time it was. So I told him, and he accepted it. You've got to believe that, because it's true.' The anguish in her voice was suddenly retreating.

During the silence that followed, the tension in the young woman's body also seemed to evaporate. Slowly her head lowered and her gaze with it before she spoke again. 'Perhaps its better this way, because I don't think I could have stood it much longer.' She drew in breath painfully. 'I might as well tell you. Nobody murdered Angela. It . . . it was an accident.'

The last sentence had come almost in a whisper.

'I don't believe it could have been an accident, Kate,' Treasure said flatly. 'But why don't you sit down and tell me about it?' He had moved to her side and pulled out a chair from the table, allowing her to sink into it.

At first she said nothing, but silently started to weep. She had buried her face in her hands.

'If Nigel Cudlum persuaded you to be his accomplice, it'd be better to admit it now.' As Treasure spoke, he sat himself on the other side of the table. 'You see, if your involvement was simply—'

'Stop it! Stop it!' Her arms thumped to the table. Her tear-stained face lifted briefly so that he caught the capitulation in the eyes. 'I've said already, it had nothing to do with Nigel. If he's said anything, he's guessing. To protect me. It was fate, that's all. An accident, I tell you . . . When we were leaving the basement.'

'You and Mrs Cudlum?'

'Yes. Angela and me.'

'You'll have to tell it from there for the police statement. You understand?'

'Yes,' she almost whispered.

She seemed hardly to have registered the entry of Detective Inspector Daynon accompanied by a younger man.

Chapter Nineteen

'It was after the American left. Marvin Smurt. After he left Angela. That's when I went down to the basement,' Kate Garely was continuing her halting account some minutes later. She had stopped weeping. Her voice seemed strangely detached, but she was having trouble with con-centration. Dully, she watched as the younger policeman, a round-faced man, introduced as Detective Sergeant Hardy, took a note of what she had just said. He was seated to her right.

'That would have been at exactly ten o'clock, Miss Garely?' asked Daynon. He was opposite her, beside Treasure, on the long side of the table.

'I expect so. I'm not sure. About then. I'd been here. In the kitchen. Tidying up for Angela.' Her brow knitted with the obvious effort of recall. 'Then I collected my coat and went down. I told her Nigel was home. He was with Lancelot Tinder in the study. I'd heard Mr Tinder arrive just before.'

'Did either Reverend Cudlum or Mr Tinder see you, miss?' Sergeant Hardy put in, a touch of Wiltshire or Hampshire in the voice.

She shook her head. 'Smurt had upset Angela. I told her to forget him. To stop what she was doing. To come for a drink with the others. In the Bell and Hammer. She said she would. So we left.'

'By the door to the steps outside, not through the vicarage?' This was Daynon.

'Yes.' She turned her gaze from Hardy back to him. 'It

was while she was trying to lock the door behind us— '

'Trying?' Daynon interrupted.

'It was sticking. She had to bang it to, very hard. It was then, for some reason, she remembered she hadn't paid me for the ham.' Her hands came up to cup her fraught face as the words stopped – as though to mark an especially distressing memory.

'The ham, miss?' It was the detective sergeant who did the prompting this time.

She was silent for several seconds more, then she took a breath and exhaled it slowly. 'Angela had asked me to buy the ham. To make sandwiches for us, before the meeting. I said I didn't want the money. She insisted. Took it from her purse. I was still refusing when she forced it on me. Into my hand. I was wearing gloves. I dropped a pound coin. We thought it had slipped between the bottom step and the wall. Angela said she'd fish it out with the knife.'

'Which knife would that have been, miss?'

'It was Marlon's. Marlon Barclay. He must have dropped it. She'd picked it up as we were leaving. I saw her open it. She told me to go back and put the porch light on again. So she could see what she was doing. The key was still in the lock. I opened the door. It was very stiff. I had to push it. Then I put on the light. The switch is just inside. And that's when I heard the noise.'

'What sort of noise, Miss Garely?' asked Daynon.

'Of something sliding. Something heavy. I thought it was in the street above.' She shuddered. 'Then they started hitting the ground. One after the other.'

'What did?'

'The slates. From the roof of the big porch.'

'D'you think they came loose through your both having to shake the door, Kate?' Treasure put in quickly and pointedly.

'I don't know. I only know I was safe inside when I saw one of them hit Angela. It was a freak. A freak thing to happen,' she repeated. 'She was bent right over, looking

209

for the coin. The slate went straight into her neck. Like an axe. You wouldn't believe. She gave a groan. Only a little one. Then she slipped forward on the step. But her head was more . . . more forward than her body. It was hanging. Like . . . like a broken doll's head.'

There was a momentary grave silence.

'And was the slate still bedded in her neck, Miss Garely?' This was Daynon.

'Yes. The slate was still . . . still there. Because it was sort of held by the step.' The young woman's face was drained of all colour now. She was sitting quite motionless. Her voice was entirely without expression, but she was having less trouble than before in finding words. 'And I'm sure now Angela was dead.'

'But did you do anything to her?'

She swallowed with effort before replying. 'When I went to her, when I saw her close to, I had a terrible premonition. If she wasn't dead, if she survived, she'd be an invalid for ever. On her back. Helpless. Do you understand?' She looked from face to face. 'I knew someone just like that. Someone who'd rather have died. It was after a skiing accident.' The words stopped as the speaker's eyes seemed to glaze even more. She took another deep breath. 'That was why I had to make sure,' she completed, and once more tears were evidently welling inside her.

'So you pushed the slate harder into the neck?' Daynon demanded in the same cold, even brusque fashion as before.

She nodded slowly.

'To be sure both the carotid arteries were severed?' the detective inspector pressed.

'Yes,' she whispered.

'And you understood what you were doing?'

She looked up. 'I understood what I might be doing. If it hadn't been done already.'

'You didn't take her pulse?'

'No. Not then. I knew later I might have done. If I had, I don't think I could . . . You see I was thinking of

her. Of Angela. And Nigel as well. About his new job.'
The phrases had followed each other quickly. Now she
paused. No one else made to speak before she resumed,
half to herself: 'Salchester was so important to him. With an
invalid wife, he might not have been able to go there after
all.' Again, she looked at each face in turn, in a mute plea
for understanding. 'Angela had never been any help in his
work. It wasn't her fault. She hated herself for it, though.
And now he'd got the job he wanted, you could say despite
her. And she was so happy for him. If he'd had to give it up
because of her, she'd . . . she'd never have forgiven herself.
Never.'

'But you understood the gravity of your action, Miss
Garely?'

'I knew some people might say it was wrong. If they knew
what I'd done. I knew that the second after I'd done it. But
she was dead. I'm sure she was dead before . . . before I.'
She drew in her breath sharply.

'So why didn't you report what had happened?'

After a long pause she answered. 'I thought it'd be
better if someone else found her.'

'Because of what you'd done.' This came as a comment
not a question from Daynon.

'I suppose so.'

'Hoping it would be taken for an accident? To avoid
suspicion?'

'Yes,' she answered him, this time more abruptly.

'So you went back through the door, miss? Locking it
on the inside?' asked Hardy, without looking up from his
pen and notebook.

'I had Angela's key.'

'D'you have it still, miss?'

'No. I got rid of it. Next day.'

'How, miss?'

'I dropped it down a drain.'

'And what did you do next? After you'd locked the
door?' This was Daynon.

211

'I've told you that already. I left through the vicarage. I met the others in the pub.'

'And why did you subsequently try twice to implicate Mr Frakraj?'

'Only after the inquest. Not before. When it came out about . . . about the second lot of pressure on the slate. That they thought it was murder. I hadn't expected that. I panicked.'

'Because you thought you'd be suspected? Or because you were afraid someone else might be?' demanded Daynon, leaning forward towards her as she spoke.

Again she took some time before replying. 'Because someone else might be.'

'Who, Miss Garely.'

She didn't answer.

'Was it Mr Cudlum?'

'It might have been.'

The two detectives exchanged glances.

'Was that because of the insurance he had on Mrs Cudlum's life?' Daynon pressed.

She shook her head. 'Because she'd told me she was ready to leave him for good. If things didn't work out in Salchester. Because she didn't want to risk being in his way any more. I thought if she'd told anyone else that, and it got to the police, you wouldn't understand. You could think she was deserting him just at the time he'd need a wife most. That Nigel might have killed her to stop her humiliating him once again.' She brought her hands and forearms tightly together over her breasts. 'Oh, I don't know what I was thinking. I only wanted to protect him. From being accused of something I'd done.'

'Are you in love with Mr Cudlum?' This was Daynon again.

She lifted her head slowly. 'Yes, I love him. But we aren't lovers, if that's what you mean.'

'But did you expect to marry him after Mrs Cudlum died?'

'That's not why I did it. It was for her sake.'

'But you'd arranged to move to Salchester yourself?'

'That was for her too. Because she begged me. To help them both. It's what I've always tried to do here. To make up for what she lacked. To help his career.'

Daynon nodded at the sergeant who said: 'We still need to know why you tried to implicate Mr Frakraj, miss.'

'Because when you were asking everyone questions, he was the one you concentrated on. I knew there couldn't be enough evidence against him in the end. But I thought it would keep suspicion away from me.'

'And from Mr Cudlum?'

'Perhaps.'

'And it was you who set up Mr Frakraj in the cemetery?'

'Yes.'

'You alone?'

'Yes.'

There was a brief silence before Daynon asked: 'About your moving forward the time the three of you ate? You knew the importance of that when it came to establishing the time of death?'

'I . . . I knew enough, yes.'

'Of course, she knew life couldn't be sustained once both carotid arteries were cut,' said Treasure. He and Molly were tracing their way through the nearly deserted Georgian streets of Bath, towards their hotel in the Royal Crescent.

It was four months after the confrontation in the St Martin's vicarage, and close to midnight on a moonlit Friday in June. The night was balmy and still, with the scent of blossom from the nearby park hanging in the air. Molly was appearing at the Theatre Royal in a short, prior-to-London tour of an early Noël Coward play. Treasure had driven down to be with her for the weekend. They had just eaten well at Clos du Roy in George Street. The trial of Kate Garely had ended at the Old Bailey the day before.

'But it said in the paper there was a conflict of medical

213

evidence.' Molly threaded her arm through his as they turned into Gay Street.

'Thanks to the expert medical witness produced by her counsel. He challenged the autopsy report and the coroner's verdict. He contended no one could be absolutely certain the arteries weren't severed by the first thrust of that slate. The jury must have agreed with him. It's why she was acquitted.'

'But you don't think she should have been?'

He shrugged. 'If the prosecution had gone for manslaughter instead of murder, the jury might not have been so lenient.'

'But she did confess, after all.'

'Not to murder she didn't. In fact, in the end, her counsel made her retract most of that first police statement. She pleaded not guilty to everything. Then I suppose the prosecution were too confident they'd get a conviction for murder. She was certainly guilty of something.'

'Even if she dug the slate in out of compassion?' Molly leaned her shoulder more against his as they walked, looking up into his face. 'And you did rather fancy her, darling. At the beginning.'

'That has nothing to do with it,' he replied loftily.

'She's very attractive. And intelligent. I think you were showing good taste. On the face of it. One hardly imagined . . . ' She sniffed. 'So was she in cahoots with the Vicar, d'you think?'

'Not over the death of his wife. But I can't believe she didn't tell him what had happened afterwards. I could be wrong.'

'So he could have conspired with her to have suspicion fall on poor Mr Frakraj.'

'Possibly. But certain Frakraj would never be arrested. Just to keep the police wrong-footed till they lost interest in the case. But she may still have handled that on her own, without involving Cudlum. If he *was* in it with her, it was she who did the leading.'

'You think he's weak?'

'In that kind of situation, yes.'

'Isn't that exquisite in the moonlight?' They had stopped to admire the Circus as they entered it from the south: thirty-three houses with Greek entablatures divided into three equal arced terraces.

'John Wood's last masterpiece. Started in 1754, the year he died. Finished by his son,' Treasure provided. 'Let's go the long way round.'

As they set off anti-clockwise Molly said: 'Mrs Lodey must be delighted that Tinder is getting his comeuppence.'

'That's overstating it. She's not vindictive. His trial for embezzlement's in September.'

'But he's repaid the money?'

'Most of it. Thanks to a killing he made in oil futures. That was after the Middle East upset in March. Doesn't alter the Crown Prosecutor's intention to make an example of him. Quite right too,' the banker concluded severely. 'Lawyers and accountants who steal from clients should all be jailed.'

'Yes, darling.'

'He's resigned from the council, of course. And from all those church appointments. I gather Mrs Lodey and Miss Modd are being a great comfort to his wife. And the daughter.'

'Caroline? I didn't tell you she wrote to me here about her engagement to Peter Windle. Now there's a young man who's not afraid to buck convention.'

'By having a future father-in-law on bail pending trial? Hmm. I think he's aware Akro Aziz was pretty decent about giving him promotion. After his loyalty had been put in question. Maybe he's taken a lesson in tolerance as a result.'

'Was the disloyalty over his connection with the Investors for Jesus? I thought that wasn't proved?'

'It was proven because he had the good sense to admit it to a superior himself, before it leaked in any other way.

215

You realise, if it hadn't been for him, the Investors wouldn't have got an early alert that Saint Martin's might be coming up for grabs? That was supposed to be an Aziz exclusive, courtesy of Tinder. Windle let it out inadvertently he says. When he was being interviewed for a job with the Investors early last year.'

'I'm glad he owned up.' They had left the Circus and were strolling along Brock Street when Molly mused: 'I still feel sorry for Marvin Smurt.'

'That buffoon? He hasn't come to any harm,' Treasure replied as though regretting the fact.

'But you said he'd been demoted and sent home.'

'By Jethro Tanglewood, who's sorry he ever sent him here.'

'That's Brother Jethro?'

'Yes, splendid chap. Came to see me at the end of last week. The day after he got in from Chicago. He'd already been to see the Area Bishop, the Archdeacon, Acro Aziz, and the Secretary of the Church Commissioners. They didn't know what had hit them. As a matter of fact, I didn't either,' he grinned.

'And he'd fixed this deal already?'

'By the end of this week he had. Good as. It's been left to the bank to tie up, but he got signatures on documents of intent, plus everyone's solemn word before he went back to the States.'

'So how did he do it all so quickly? You said doing anything with a redundant church would take years.'

Treasure chuckled again. 'He bribed everyone involved.'

'Including the Bishop?'

'Especially the Bishop. Not that anyone gets anything personal out of it, of course. But what Jethro was offering was an irresistible deal. Everyone thought so. Including Mrs Lodey in the end. But he put a time limit on acceptance.'

'How long?'

'Noon last Wednesday. Or the whole thing was off.

216

It just shows the Church of England can move as fast as anyone else if you offer the right bait.'

'So Aziz Developments get the church site,' said Molly flatly.

'But the diocese gets a nine hundred and ninety-nine year lease on the basement for nothing. Or a section of the new basement slightly bigger than the present one, with fitments as required.'

'Meaning it'll be fitted out as a club again?'

'But much better than now. With a proper kitchen, loos, and so on. Oh, and with a piece partitioned off as a chapel. A modern hall for the use of all the churches in the deanery, in a very central spot.'

'So there'll still be a Sunday Club. But the diocese will get less money for the site than it would otherwise?'

'No, it's getting more. Much more. Aziz are paying the same price as the Investors were ready to offer. That's a million pounds more than Aziz was in for originally.'

'But with something deducted because of the basement?'

'No, nothing. The Investors will buy the basement from Aziz, and give it to the diocese.'

'Thanks to the benevolence of Brother Jethro?' Molly sounded impressed. 'So what are the Investors for Jesus getting out of it?'

'A disused parish hall in Shepherd's Bush. One the Church Commissioners haven't been able to shift. The Investors are paying a fair price for it. It's an area zoned for light industrial use only.'

'But closer to the BBC than Saint Martin's?'

'Precisely. Much better all round for them, and at a fraction of the cost.'

'So why buy the Saint Martin's basement and give it away? That must be expensive?'

'Not in terms of what Jethro Tanglewood calls positive public relations. It seems the Investors have been getting a bad image in the States. For unjustifiable reasons, so far as I can see. For instance, they're not involved in insider trading. They're just fast and intelligent analysts of market information when they get it.'

'Or so Brother Jethro says?'

'Yes. But I believe him. Or I believe him sufficiently.'

'Or you wouldn't have accepted the Investors as customers of Grenwood, Phipps?'

'Sure. And there are no conflicts of interest now with other customers. Anyway, they're working on their public image at home, and they want to get it right from the start in Europe.'

'And setting up a new Sunday Club fits?'

'When it's announced formally. It should generate more free press and television coverage than the same expenditure would buy in advertising space. Jethro plans to be here for the announcement.'

'Isn't that some kind of exploitation?'

'If you want to use an emotive word, yes, it is. You could also call it sponsorship, I suppose. Or even a charitable action.'

'For an ulterior motive.'

Treasure shrugged. 'Everyone involved seems to be benefiting from the deal. Not least the members of the Sunday Club.'

Molly pondered for a moment. 'Nine hundred and ninety-nine years is a very long time.'

'See us all out,' he replied, with a grin.

'But Saint Martin's will be knocked down?'

They were in the Royal Crescent, arguably the most serene Georgian terrace in England, and most especially so when bathed in moonlight. Molly had led them across the road to where they were now standing, to look down over the wide expanse of park that swooped below.

'It's not as if an important part of the national heritage is being destroyed,' said Treasure. 'Saint Martin's has really very little to commend it. And it's falling to pieces in any case.' He turned about to admire the elegant, well-proportioned houses that made up the crescent. His foot had been resting on the coping of a low wall, as old as the crescent itself. As he moved, he dislodged a sliver of Bath stone which fell away onto the pavement.

They both solemnly regarded the damage.

'I'll agree about Saint Martin's,' said Molly. 'So long as you promise not to tell Brother Jethro that the City of Bath is disintegrating.'